NIGHTOUT

SIYA'S
NIGHTOUT

Be Careful for What the Night Might Await...

J. SAHANI

Notion Press

Old No. 38, New No. 6
McNichols Road, Chetpet
Chennai - 600 031

First Published by Notion Press 2016
Copyright © J. Sahani 2016
All Rights Reserved.

ISBN 978-1-945926-65-5

For my Grandma,
who told me endless stories whenever I demanded

CONTENTS

CONTENTS

SIYA

"Bye mom!" said Siya, and rushed for her school bus. Again she was late today, as usual. Somehow she caught the bus. "Caught it at the last moment," she said panting.

"Hi!" said the girl sitting next to her.

"Hello Sharda!" Siya replied cheerfully, taking a breath of relief.

"Did we get any homework for Chemistry?" Sharda asked, looking puzzled. "'coz I haven't done anything and some of the genius heads like Nihar, DJ (a nickname of Dibyajyoti) and Lakshmi say that we had to complete worksheet 3 of Structure of Atoms. I really don't remember Vaishnavi Ma'am talking anything about homework, you know."

"You were actually dozing in Chemistry class," said Siya.

"Again?"

Siya nodded and took out her Chemistry notebook from her bag. "Here," said she, handing out the notebook to Sharda. "Complete the homework and give it to me before lunch." Siya said with a smile. "We have the chemistry period just after lunch."

"Thankyou so very much, Siya. I'll complete it as soon as possible," Sharda promised. Sharda had almost started writing: *Worksheet 3 2.1) Magnesium's valency is 2, therefore —*

"Now, come on. We've reached school." Saying so, Siya hopped down from the bus amidst the hustle and bustle of students from all classes. Sharda hurriedly closed the notebooks on her lap and stuffed them into her bag. She was the last one to come out of the bus. Siya climbed up the stairs to the second floor and walked into her class VIII C.

"Morning Anika!" said Siya, springing her schoolbag under her desk.

"Good Morning!" her best friend Anika returned the greeting, busy arranging her books and notebooks according to the Thursday timetable.

"I bet Sharda will again fall asleep today in someone's class," said Siya. "History, most probably."

"What are you talking about Sharda? Raveena ma'am is so boring that the whole class starts yawning, and half of the class totally slumbers, only except you who remains as alert as a watchdog!"

"That's not true! Even I find her boring. But just in case she might call out some important notes, I try to listen to her." Siya tried to explain.

"Yeah! That's actually good for me anyways, because at the end of the day, I just have to copy the notes from you."

"Hmm," was all that Siya replied.

"And talking about Sharda, I'm sure Rehman Sir will again offer to gift her a pillow in the next bio class."

"True!" Siya agreed with a giggle.

"Look who's coming to flirt you," Anika teased, elbowing Siya. "I'm telling this guy has a crush on you."

"Shut up! He's the most idiotic person I've ever seen on earth." Siya remarked with a blush and a frown coming on her face at the same time.

"Hi Miss Genius! How many books did you complete yesterday, and how many are you planning to read today? How much tension do you give to the teachers? Shame on you! If you don't study, then it will be so easy for the teachers to give you a zero in your answer sheets!!"

"Why are you so interested in Siya, anyways?" Anika asked immediately, in a sing-song voice.

Abhilash turned red. "I...um...I just..." Abhilash turned redder and redder, searching for an answer to this. Just then, the bell rang. "Assembly time, girls." Saying this, he instantly walked away.

"I'm telling you Abhilash is mad for you." Anika said.

"Shut up." said Siya.

"No really, he –

"Shut up!" Siya repeated, cutting Anika halfway through her sentence. They walked down through the corridors to the huge assembly hall where the whole school was gathered. Siya joined her usual place in the choir, and Anika fell into line with the other eighthers. They started singing the morning prayer 'Humko man ki shakti dena' with Siya and seven other girls in the lead. It was just another day of usual school. The same eight periods, from which just one period was a non-study time: library, the only interesting study period: English, and SST (Social Studies), of course, as Anika put it – "**S**tudents **S**leeping **T**ime."

Siya was the top of their class, as well as a talented and caring girl. As all the other parents put it: She was just *perfect*! Yet, as everyone has a plus and a minus, she too had some negatives. She had two main cons in her life. First, she found it too difficult to be obedient, especially to her parents. For example, that day when she returned home, she threw her bag, her shoes and changed her dress. Then she rushed to the drawing room and switched on the TV. It was the time for her favourite show.

"Keep your shoes in the shoe stand and your clothes in the cupboard. Things should be kept in their proper place dear," advised Mrs. Sharma.

"That's not important, Mom."

"It is. It will take you just a minute or two."

"Oh Mom! I don't want to miss even a glance of this episode. I can do all that stupid stuff afterwards."

"But you'll forget. I know that very well."

"No mom, this time I won't forget."

"Oh really? Well, you say that every time. Don't show your tantrums. GO and DO it right NOW!" Siya's mom ordered.

"I won't," Siya protested.

"Go means go."

"No means NO. If you want it to be done, then why don't you do it yourself? This is my show time, and I WILL see it." She slammed the door, and stalked out.

"What an irritating child! Never listens to a word of mine."

And second, she couldn't trust anyone easily. This was her strength as well as her weakness. This was the reason for which she could get as loyal a friend as Anika. But this was also the reason for which she had a very few friends, whom she could call 'close friends' and 'real friends'.

ANIKA COMES HOME

Saturday evening. Now Siya was supposed to be playing tennis. Instead, she was doing her homework. Unable to concentrate, she watched through the glass of her window. She observed the tiny transparent drops of water falling casually and continuously from the sky, unable to find anything else more interesting than that. She cursed the clouds for the thousandth time for showering rain in her playtime and making her day so boring.

After some time, Siya's mom called her. As she was anyways not interested in studying at the present moment, she did not take a second to obey her mother and sprinted down the curved stairs. Siya was surprised to see luggages and her parents dressed up.

"Dad, are you going somewhere?" asked Siya.

"We're going to your grandma's house," said Mr. Sharma.

"She's ill, Siya. She has no one to look after her. We must go," answered Mrs. Sharma before Siya could ask 'why?' which she was about to ask and had just opened her mouth, and then abruptly closed it.

Siya felt sorry for her sweet grandma. "I too want to come with you," she requested.

"No sweetheart, your exams are just a fortnight ahead," said Mrs. Sharma. "Now you are a grown up. You are big enough to take care of yourself. It's time that you became responsible."

"We'll be back as soon as possible," asserted Mrs. Sharma. Siya didn't protest anymore, suddenly realizing the advantage in this. She smiled to herself surreptitiously.

Siya touched the feet of her parents.

"*Ayushmati bhawa*(Live long)!" Her parents blessed her.

"Convey my regards to grandma. I know she'll be well," said Siya, determined.

"Yes Siya, sure," affirmed Mrs. Sharma with the same determination.

Mrs. Sharma was just about to leave, when she came back and said, "Siya, do whatever you like to, but don't go to the storeroom. It's dangerous. Okay?"

"Yes mom," said Siya. "Goodnight!"

"That's what she says me every time she leaves me alone at home," thought Siya. "And of course, the reason of this danger would be some big rats with large white teeth, that's what she says me every time I ask **'why'** and makes her eyes as scary as if she has just seen a cobra."

"And don't invite friends," said Mrs. Sharma. "Not when there's no one in the house, and I also don't like it much."

"Yes mom," said Siya sulkily. "Problems like what?" she wanted to ask, but didn't. "And she says *this* too," thought Siya miserably, "Everytime! *Everytime!*"

"We will soon be back, dear." Mr. Sharma hugged Siya as he bid her goodbye.

"Take care, darling." Mrs. Sharma planted a soft kiss on Siya's forehead, and left the house with Mr. Sharma.

Siya quickly shut the door and ran to the balcony to see her parents leaving in their car. She waved a grand goodbye to her parents, and as soon as they left, Siya started dancing and shouting and leaping with joy. Her parents leaving her alone in the house meant only one thing to Siya -freedom. Now no one would restrict her. She felt like the master of the house.

She spent the rest of the day watching TV, playing video games, and chatting online with her friends.

Siya looked at the clock. Now it was 10:30. Siya texted Anika.

Siya: Sorry Anika. I know that I am disturbing you by calling at this time of night.

Anika: Not at all, silly. Never mind. Tell me, what are you doing?

Siya: Well, I was just wondering if you could come to my house. We'll have a late night party and enjoy ourselves.

Anika: (shocked) Are you crazy? I mean, yes of course I can come. As you know, I leave with my elder brother and he won't mind a bit. He's always carefree. But what about your mom? She's sweet, but she's strict too! Won't she get mad at us?

Siya: Don't worry, you just come here. Waiting for you. Bye. TTYL!

Anika: Okay. Coming.

Anika wrote a message for her brother and left it in her brother's bedroom by slipping the paper through the gap between the floor and the room's door. She rode her bicycle and started for Siya's house.

The road was desolate and everything was silent. Anika could hear a faint noise of footsteps from far behind her. She stopped to make certain that no one was there. But now, she couldn't hear anything. It was all silent again. A tiny sound broke the silence. Anika found out that the sound was from her bicycle. The tyre of the bicycle creaked again. She looked around to make sure, which brought her to the conclusion that she was being looked upon by a dozen of spectators. The spectators were the streetlights which were continuously glaring at her. Anika still had a feeling that there was someone there. Was someone following her? That was silly. So she didn't strain her ears anymore and pedalled her way straight to Siya's house.

Within five minutes, Anika was at the door of Siya's house, ringing the doorbell, only to find that the door was already open for her welcome.

"Siya, are you sure that Aunty won't be angry?" Anika asked uncertainly. Siya grinned. "Mom and Daddy have gone to pay a visit to grandma, and they have left me alone!" Siya said squealing. Her eyes were glittering with excitement. This took away all the tension from Anika's head at once.

TELL ME A SECRET

"As much as I can guess, my parents will most probably return around seven o'clock or seven thirty." Siya declared, as she sat up on her table. "And tomorrow is Sunday. So it brings us to the conclusion that we have a total of almost 18 hours together," announced Siya. "So the ...time starts ....NOW. And it'll end tomorrow at six o'clock."

They discussed whether to play video games, or watch a movie or call their friends for a late night party & overnight stay. They debated over the topic for a while. But they finally decided that casually gossiping would be a much more better option.

So, they talked and joked and laughed and ended up pillow fighting.

"We're best friends, right? Today, let's share some secrets of our lives," said Siya

"OK. Tell me your secret," said Anika

"You say."

"You first!"

"No, you"

"But it was your suggestion."

"You, you, you"

"Ok – Ok! me, me, me"

"Yes!" Siya made the victory.

"But then, what secret do you want me to tell you?" asked Anika. "Let me think if I have any secret at all … secret … secret … secret … Yes! Today I had sandwich in my breakfast."

"What's the secret in it?" asked Siya, narrowing her eyes.

"A secret is something about which you don't know, right? So I said you something which was unknown to you. Simple."

"Oh God! Anika! Tell me an interesting secret."

"I was just joking," said Anika.

"I know that. But the thing is that, I didn't find your joke very funny."

"Ok then, I'll tell you a secret. But you'll have to promise that you won't say about it to anyone," requested Anika.

"But I was planning to post it on facebook and make the whole world know about your secret!"

"Jokes apart. But please, I really want you to promise me that you won't say this to anyone. Just as a precaution to avoid you saying it by chance..like…just in case you let this out by a slip of toungue. So promise me."

"Oh God! Anika!" Siya rolled her eyes. "Fine! I swear. I won't say anyone," promised Siya.

"Well…umm..It's like this……"

"Anika, will you even tell something or just go like "um…" and "well…" and stuff?"

"Okay. Fine. So the secret is that I think Mohit has got a crush on me."

"I …I knew it. I JUST TOTALLY KNEW IT!!! OMG!" By now, Siya was literally dancing and rolling madly.

"Don't shout, silly. And what do you name that dance which you just presented?"

"Oh my God. I know I am acting totally crazy, but presently I am just bursting with ecstatic excitement."

"I can see that," said Anika.

"But surely, it's not only him who is in love. As much as I have studied you since last year, I'm pretty sure that you too have got feelings for that guy."

Anika blushed.

"Oh no. That's nonsense," said Anika, her face as pink as the rose in Siya's balcony. "I mean, okay. He is a nice boy. But.."

"Now come on Anika," Siya urged. "You can't hide your feelings from your best friend. I have known you since nursery. I had seen that glow in your eyes when you had seen Mohit looking at you on the first day of this session. I have…"

"Okay, okay, okay. Enough of this lovey-dovey talk. What about you? I think Abhilash likes you."

"What?"

"Or even better, maybe you like Abhilash?"

Now, the way Siya's face turned red from all laughter to all anger was a sight of transformation worth seeing. "What did you say? That idiot! That stupid fool! That bloody moron! How the heck could you even think of me liking him? You son of a bitch!"

Now it was the turn of Anika to take the fun. "I'm a girl, dude. It should be 'daughter of a bitch'," Anika said coolly.

"SHUT UP!!!!"

The fun went on for some more time. Finally Anika ended it by saying, "Now it's your turn."

"Hmmm. My secret is that.........you are not my best friend."

"Bad joke," Anika responded.

"No really. Yes, you are a nice friend, but not best friend."

"Uhh...okay. But I thought it was you who had decided that we were best friends." Anika couldn't think of anything else to say. She was filled with shock and surprise and disgust.

"Well, yes. But that was a long time ago. I don't think that I like you anymore. I mean, don't feel bad, but maybe, it was after all not such a good idea to make you my best friend. You see, our ideas and hobbies don't really match."

Anika didn't respond to this. She was speechless.

Then Siya smiled. "Because you know what? I don't just like you, I LOVE you! And you are not my best friend, you are my BFF – my best friend forever!"

Anika couldn't stop smiling. "You bitch, come here! I'll not leave you today." But she couldn't catch Siya, Siya was already running. "So this was you secret, isn't it?" They ran and ran and laughed until their sides ached.

"Now, tell me a proper secret," demanded Anika.

"I ate bread toast and boiled eggs in my breakfast."

"Hahaha. Very funny," said Anika.

"Cool, I'll tell you a secret," said Siya. "Come with me."

THE UNKNOWN CORNER

"Where are you taking me? I never came to this side of the house," said Anika, surprised.

"This is the dark side of our house," said Siya in a cunning, scary way.

"There must be a light bulb somewhere," said Anika looking around, as the corridors began began becoming darker and darker with their every step.

"You won't find a flicker of light in this place," went on Siya in the same scary tone.

"Hey! Do you think I'm a kid of five who is going to be scared by your silly stories? Now don't cook up a tale and go –

There was once an old rich lady who owned this enormous palace like building. But one dark night, as of today, a close blood relative deceived her and murdered her to get his hand on all her properties and money, and then sold this building to my (Siya's) family. Burning in rage, the old lady uttered the words- I'll take revenge before taking my last breath. It is believed that the old woman's soul still haunts the house in this area. Today is the 50th death anniversary of –" Anika was going to continue mimicking Siya's voice when, "Stop it Anika, please shut up. I'm not joking," said Siya. "You see that room?"

"Yeah, anything special about that room?" asked Anika, not thinking it to be serious at all.

"A lot. It holds the biggest secret of our family. I've been kept in suspense about this secret all my life."

"What secret? You mean, you yourself don't know what the secret is?"

"You are right. I myself don't know what's so extra ordinary about this store room and why my mom keeps warning me about this room every time she leaves me alone at home," said Siya.

"Do you think the treasure box contains a poisonous snake guarding its precious jewels and diamonds, waiting to throw its fangs on any culprit who dares to open the treasure box?" guessed Anika.

"Or will it be kind of ghostly, as it says in books? Like... 'At the strike of midnight, the evil awakened and so ...'" Siya guessed further.

"Maybe the box contains a witch trapped in it."

"And maybe there are thousands of moths and ugly insects in it."

"Or ......, it maybe simply some test papers of your mother or father, if in case they scored bad marks by any chance."

"It can be anything," said Siya. "Let's not be in this suspense anymore. Let's reveal the secret all by ourselves."

"OK. So our **'what's the secret'** mission starts now."

"This way." Siya led Anika to the door of the store room.

"Do you see that?" asked Siya.

"Yes. But I see something else too," said Anika.

"What else do you see?" asked Siya curiously.

"There. Do you understand now what I mean?"

Siya glanced to where Anika was pointing and immediately her expression changed "Oh God. Nooooooo!"

WHAT NEXT?

The door was locked.

"This shouldn't have happened!" continued Siya –
"The door shouldn't have been locked. It really shouldn't.
Oh dear, I was so keen to know about the secrets that
this room held. But now it's impossible. I mean. This is
so unfair.

"Yes, this door's colour is very dark," said Anika,
mimicking a thoughtful and serious tone.

"Don't joke! I am serious. This really shouldn't have
happened. It –

"Shut up, Siya. Do you think the door will open if
you keeps on critisizng our luck? Let's think of something!
There must be some way or the other to enter. I just wish
the door could open if I say *'Khul Ja sim sim'* (Open sim
sim) as in Alibaba and the forty thieves."

"Well, that's not possible," Anika said.

Anika was not talented like Siya who always topped
the class, but she was way ahead of her in dealing with
practical day to day life issues.

"Is there any window or something sort of that?"

"No, I don't think so, as I've never seen one for this room," answered Siya. "Oh, my hair! It's falling on my eyes." She adjusted her hair by putting the front bunch of stands behind her ear. "Another hair pin or two would have been perfect."

Suddenly, Anika's eyes broadened. "Thank you, there you are! You got it. You are a brilliant thinker." Anika's words were tumbling out with both excitement and joy.

"But what did I think of?" asked Siya, bewildered.

"You'll come to know about that in a minute," said Anika. "You just give me your hairpin."

"There you are," obeyed Siya, still confused.

Anika made a shape by bending the hair pin and put the remoulded hair pin into the hole, and tried to open it. Now Siya understood what Anika was doing, and smiled.

She tried and tried but all in vain. She squeezed the ends of the pin a bit more, and again tried, but failed. She tried for a third time, fourth time and fifth.

Now she was frustrated. "I give up," said Anika frustrated. "You were right, this is simply impossible."

"Now come on, Anika. Nothing is impossible, and you know that. One should never give up. Come on, give it a try once more. I'm sure you can do it."

"Ok, if you say this is possible, then maybe it is possible after all." Anika decided to try once again. But again she failed. She tried again. A slight click sound was heard, as the hairpin moved through the hole. Anika moved the hairpin further and a circle of total 360 degree was completed by the hairpin, through the hole of the lock. Finally, the lock was opened. They had achieved their first success in their mission.

They took out the lock and opened the door. The entrance of the room led their view to a dingy dark room where nothing, not a single thing was visible. As they tried to walk, they stumbled down by a lot of stuff which felt to their skin like books, papers, broken pieces of glass, broken parts of machines and vehicles, etc., etc..

"Ew! What's this?" said Siya. Anika took out her cell phone and switched on the torch to enquire what had made her friend feel like that. "I hate that thing," Siya murmured.

"It's just a spider web dude," said Anika, laughing. "It's no monster going to swallow you!"

"I don't like spider webs or spiders. In fact, I hate every species belonging to phylum arthropoda," said Siya. "With butterfly, of course, as an exception."

"Here is a stick," Anika said assuredly. "I'll tear this web out." Siya was awkwardly fiddling with her hair, watching Anika efficiently and casually removing the web with the stick, as if that was the easiest thing to do in the world. "Here we go. Let's go further and see what we can find there."

"Okay, let's go. And thank you for the spider web thing."

"Don't mention it," Anika replied with a smile. "I didn't know that this store room is so large and long. In fact, I had never walked in such a large storeroom."

"Even I am surprised about this. I never came here before."

"Ouch!" Siya tripped over something and fell down; something hard and rough, it seemed to be a rock.

"Hey, careful! You okay?" Anika asked as she helped Siya to her feet.

"Yeah" Siya got up, wondering what had made her trip and fall like that.

"How idiotic!" thought Siya, disgusted with herself. "Am I that clumsy?"

"Weird. I never saw you fall over anything. You were like the most sophisticated and graceful and poised model of the class."

"Well, maybe I was unmindful. I wish I had super powerful eyes, with which I could see in the dark too. Your torch is useless! It can't even properly light up a puppy's ken."

"Well, I'm sure no dog would even feel the need of it," said Anika. Just then there was a slight sound, as if some metal object had fallen on the ground.

"Did you hear that sound?" asked Siya instantly.

"What sound?" Anika did not have as active sense organs as Siya.

"Never mind, maybe it was just my imagination."

"We should have brought a torch with us. Only If I had any idea that the store house would be pitch black like this," said Anika.

"Let me see if I have my cell phone in my skirt pocket. As much as I know, my mobile's torch glows as bright as a lantern."

"I hope against hope that you do have it." Anika said as she cross fingered both her hands.

MOVE ON

Siya scrambled through her left pocket, which consisted of a hundred rupee note, and then the right pocket. "Yes!" Siya exclaimed as she took out her cell phone.

"Thanks God," Anika sighed with relief. "Now, I won't have to waste my phone's battery." Siya quickly switched on the torch of her cell phone.

"My battery isn't any high either. It won't work for a long time," said Siya.

"Hmm"

They searched for something interesting in the room, but were not much successful. Most of what they saw was just the dark mosaic floor on which they were walking.

They walked for some time in silence.

"What do you expect to find here?" asked Anika, not liking the silence very much.

"I don't know. I don't want to make any guesses. Guesses rarely come true. I just want to know whatever is here in real," answered Siya.

"Hmm"

They walked for another two minutes in silence in the flickering light of the mobile torch, not really seeing what was there in the surroundings.

"Yesterday's classes were very interesting. We didn't have much to study."

"Yeah, I liked the bio activity." Anika added.

"It was a relief that our history-civics teacher was absent. That's such a boring subject!"

"Exactly. Why do we need to know if Akbar ruled in fourteenth century or twelfth century, and that Humayun was Akbar's son? These people have been dead long ago," commented Anika.

"But I think Akbar was the emperor during sixteenth century. And Humayun was Akbar's father, not his son. Jahangir was Akbar's son," corrected Siya

"Oh whatever! Who cares?" Anika had no interest in knowing who was who.

"My mobile's battery is very low. I'm switching it off, or else there won't be any light when we might be really in need."

"Right, switch it off."

They continued to move, just like that. They had no idea where they were going. They went on and on. This place seemed strangely never-ending. They kept on moving, unknown and unsure of what might happen next.

SHE'S ALRIGHT

"Damn the network!" cursed Mrs. Sharma, dialling Siya's number for the nineth time in a row, to which a the same monotonous voice of a lady again droned, "The number you are calling is not reachable at the moment. Please stay online or call later."

"Is it again coming not reachable?" asked Mr. Sharma.

"Yeah," said Mrs. Sharma feebly. "Have we taken the correct decision by leaving her alone at home? Will she be okay?"

"Don't worry about her. She's a responsible child. We know that very well, don't we?"

"Yes, we do. But –

"Then why worry? Let her be independent. Let her do whatever she wants to do. She'll never have a problem. And even if she does, she'll always find a solution. She's a brave girl, my daughter," said Mr. Sharma proudly.

Mrs. Sharma smiled. "Yeah. Our daughter."

'It's only a one-hour more way to your maa's house. We'll soon reach there.'

They drove along their way, away from Siya. Little did they know what was going to happen to their daughter.

WHERE ARE WE GOING?

"Oh God! I can't walk anymore." said Anika. "My legs are aching like hell."

"Come on. We can't give up just like that.

Josh na thanda hone pae

Kadam badhate chal,

Manjil teri pad chumegi

Aaj nahi to kal," Siya encouraged.

(Meaning: Don't let the enthusiasm get cold

Keep on stepping forward,

Your goal will kiss your feet

If not today, then tomorrow.)

"Well, poems and songs are nice to hear," remarked Anika. "But today I'm realizing that how difficult it is to put them into practise in real life."

"Right"

"I'm always right," said Anika.

"Right"

"I was just kidding. No one can be right always."

"Right," answered Siya again.

Anika stopped, a little taken aback, her lower jaws hanging. "Is this girl in her senses?" she thought.

"Everyone does some mistake or the other," Anika continued.

"Right"

"Now stop it, will you? What right, right, right, huh?"

"Ok left," joked Siya.

"Very funny," Anika sarcastically replied. "Where are we going?" she asked.

"No idea."

'Idhar chali main udhar chali

Jaane kahaan main kidhar chali

Aare fisal gayi…

Na jaane mujhe kya hua

Main tere sang ho chali.'" Siya started singing

(Meaning: I went here, I went there

No idea I went where

Oh I slipped……

No idea what happened to me

I remained going with you.)

"Great! You have a song for everything, don't you singing queen?"

"Right"

"Not again!" groaned Anika.

"Hahaha. Okay, I'll stop singing," said Siya, laughing.

"Oops!" cried Anika, as she stumbled and fell down.

"Are you okay?" asked Siya, concerned.

"I think so," replied Anika sulkily. "Oh God! I feel so exhausted. And it's also quite boring! This was supposed to be kind of an adventure," grunted Anika.

"R –"

"Don't say 'right' again," Anika said in an ordering tone.

"Okay, I won't. I'm also bored with my lame monotonous joke."

"Well, as I was saying, this was supposed to be an adventure kind of thing. And I have never known any adventure where you keep on walking and walking without even knowing where you are going, and there's no end to it, have you?"

Siya stopped momentarily. "That's it. Oh God! I was such an idiot! How could I not think of it before? Damn me!'

"What are you talking about?" asked Anika, confused.

"Turn back."

"But why?" asked Anika.

"Because we need to walk in the other direction."

"Oh wow! So we are returning. Yes?" Anika asked hopefully.

"No!" Siya snapped.

"Then why?"

"To check if we missed out something important on our way," said Siya. "Let me switch on my cell phone."

"I can't see anything else than black and grayish colour all around," complained Anika.

"Same here," agreed Siya.

"Ugh! I hate this place," groaned Anika. Siya took no notice of it.

Siya suddenly felt an imbalance in her body, but managed to stand when she was just about to fall. She tried to focus her mobile's light on the ground.

"Wait. What is this?" Siya saw something which did not match with the colour of the background.

"What is what?" asked Anika, unable to notice what Siya saw.

"There. That silvery object. It's shining a bit, sometimes. You see that?"

"Yeah. I don't know why, but it seems a bit familiar to me."

"Doesn't it feel like we've already come here?" asked Siya.

"Somehow I feel like I know this –

"Hey! This is the same place. I think we are moving in rounds." exclaimed Siya.

"Oh yes! I think this is the third round that we are making!" Anika said.

WE HAVE REACHED

"Get up, honey. We've reached," said Mr. Sharma.

"What?" Mrs. Sharma asked sleepily.

"Drink this water. Wake up. We have reached."

"Oh. I had fallen asleep," Mrs. Sharma realized.

"Yeah"

"Don't carry all the luggages. Give me some also."

"No, it's okay. You don't have to worry," assured Mr.Sharma.

"It's not okay. You will have back pain."

"No way. I'm way more stronger than you think of me, you know," Mr. Sharma insisted.

"That's no reason why you should carry everything, Mr. Porter. Now don't show me any more of your tantrums and do as I am saying. GIVE me the bags, NOW!"

"OKAY dear, okay. Here you are," Mr. Sharma gave up. "Remember that heavy rainfall day when you were carrying a handful of bags and had almost slipped down? If I had not come to your save and not ran to hold you in the nick of the time, then you would have broken your crown and would have been lying in the hospital for two weeks."

"I also remember that that day, I was wearing a high heel, and today I am wearing a flat slipper. Anything more to say?"

"No. You win and I lose," said Mr. Sharma.

Mrs. Sharma smiled.

Mr. Sharma smiled back. Nothing in the world for him was more beautiful than his wife's lovely smile.

IT'S MAGIC!

The two friends started investigating 'the silver object' which could not get any better specified name till now.

"What is this exactly?" Anika asked.

"What do you think am I doing? Why would I waste my time investigating this silly silver object if I already knew what it was?"

"Point"

"Damn it! This silly thing is not going to help us in any way." Cursing it, Siya let the 'the silver object' fall from her hand. It creaked a bit. Then it shone. First, just a little bit, almost ignorable. Then, a bit more. "I'm not interested in this anymore." She declared sleepily, her eyes half-closed.

"What did I tell you?" Yawning, Anika agreed readily.

Thus, Siya and Anika started walking away.

"What happened? Why did you stop?" Siya asked.

"I don't know. I just……I just had a feeling that someone was there."

"What nonsense? Whom do you expect to be in this ghostly place, that too at this time of night?"

"Yeah, maybe I'm too tired."

"But I really felt it." Anika whispered to herself. "I must have been mistaken."

"Hey! Did you notice that?" Siya asked.

"What? You also felt what I felt?"

"What did you feel?"

"Felt that someone was there?"

"Oh no silly! I was saying about the glow."

"Which glow?"

"The sparkle. The slight sparkle."

"Where? I can't see anything. It's just the same as being blind in this deadly place."

"There. Behind you."

"Wow!Wo-oooo- ow!It's… It's…"

"It's beautiful. Isn't it?"

The tiny sparkle magnified, and the magnanimous glow went on increasing and increasing until it had slowly occupied 'the silver object' with it's silver-gold translucent glow. In the meantime, it had converted the enormous eerie dark room into the brightest sparkling room that they had ever seen in their life. They remained spellbound and speechless, as what they saw after that was beyond their imagination. 'The silver object' along with its silver-gold aura, stated rising and then floated in the midair, all by itself.

"Siya, you never told me that you had brought me here to see a magic show."

"Even I'm surprised, Anika. I wonder if I'm dreaming."

THE RIDDLE

The irregular shaped 'the silver object' now changed into a round shaped silver sphere. A glowing golden line began piercing through the middle of the sphere, dividing the silver sphere, almost into two hemispheres, as if an invisible golden-coloured pencil had drawn a line on the silver sphere and some axe had chopped the same into two.

"Ahh! What are you doing Anika? Why are you pinching me?"

"Oh sorry! Very sorry! I was just checking if all this was actually happening, because now also I feel as if all this is a dream."

The upper hemisphere moved upwards, and a powerfully strong light was emitted from the inner part of the sphere, as bright and powerful as that of the Sun; it could have made a person blind. Siya and Anika had to move backwards and cover their faces so as to avoid the extremely bright radiations of the sphere.

Then a rolled half -drawing sheet sized parchment, as thick as a cardboard emerged from the sphere, and unfolded all by itself. It seemed to be millions of years old, but its glow and radiance was as fresh as that of a new leaf. It looked like a royal letter. Siya and Anika got their next startle when a booming voice read out the text on the paper. It read:

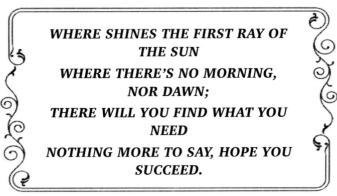

WHERE SHINES THE FIRST RAY OF THE SUN

WHERE THERE'S NO MORNING, NOR DAWN;

THERE WILL YOU FIND WHAT YOU NEED

NOTHING MORE TO SAY, HOPE YOU SUCCEED.

Saying so, the text on the paper disappeared, as if merging with thin air.

"I REPEAT,

'WHERE SHINES THE FIRST RAY OF THE SUN

WHERE THERE'S NO MORNING, NOR DAWN;

THERE WILL YOU FIND WHAT YOU NEED

NOTHING MORE TO SAY, HOPE YOU SUCCEED.'"

Saying so, the parchment rolled itself, as if programmed to do so by some automated machine. But this time, there was nothing written on it.

"How weird!" said Siya.

"Where shines the first ray of the sun? What does that mean?"

"Does that mean that we'll have to wait till morning?"

"Just check the time in your cell phone."

"Cool, wait a second."

"Yeah"

"It's three forty," Siya declared. "A.M." she added.

"Hmm"

"Do you think that place is Japan? Haven't we read in our lower classes that Japan is also known as 'Nippon' because the sun shines there the earliest?" Siya asked.

"So now you are going to Japan? Do you think Japan is some shopping mall at a five minutes distance from here? Or have you got plans to invite doremon who is going to lend you one of his anyway doors to you?"

"No, but –

Anika gave her explanation, not ready to listen to any of Siya's protests. "No, don't give me any of your 'Nothing is impossible' lectures. And if you want to go to Japan, then you're most welcome to do so. I'm not going."

"Ok, I understand."

"And even if we agree somehow that Japan is the place, then also, do you think there the people have no morning, no evening, nothing?"

"You have a point. Let's take a look on that thing once again. 'Where shines the first ray of the sun. Where there's no morning, nor dawn.' This means that whatever this place is; it's night there."

"Throughout?" Anika asked, half to herself.

"I guess so."

"But I have never heard of such a place where there's no day."

"Let's...Let's try to concentrate and think logically. I know that it's puzzling, but it must have an answer."

"Okay. One thing that I am sure by now is that magic does exist. It's not something which happens only in fictions and movies and story books. Magic is real." Anika was now assured of this.

They again had to walk in silence for some time. Siya's cell phone torch was making a brownish black hue in the ground beneath them, which she had again switched on as soon as they left the spot where the glowing hemisphere still floated in mid air.

Suddenly Siya's eyes shimmered with godly glow. Even the faint light of Siya's cell phone cum torch couldn't hide this radiance of enthusiasm. It didn't take a moment for Anika to understand that her friend had got a clue.

"That's it. I –

– got an idea." Anika completed the sentence before Siya could finish.

"Yes!" Siya did a little dance. "You only see, it's already past four. So shouldn't it have been morning already by now outside?"

"I also know that. Is that all you have discovered for which you were singing and jumping and swinging crazily?" Anika asked a little irritated.

"Patience my dear, patience," Siya answered. "*Sabr ka phal mitha hota hai, meri bachhi.*"

(Meaning: fruit of patience is sweet, my girl)

"O *mataji*, don't start your *prabochan*. Will you please take the pain to explain me what you have thought of?"

"Okay. Okay. So it's like this."

UDGHOSHAK

"Do you think it's morning, noon or evening now? Do you have any idea?"

"Of course not. It's all dark here. Your cell phone is the only source which can let us know the time," said Anika.

"Exactly! It's all dark here. It's neither morning, nor dawn. It's always night here."

"you mean this is the place?" Anika's eyes broadened

"It has to be." Siya said, determined about her discovery. "Now we have to find that spot where the first sun rays will fall."

"Now the question is, how do we find this place?"

"Want to know my plan?"

"You thought of a plan so soon?" Anika asked, amazed.

"Yes, but an extremely dumb idea, and the only way I can think of getting to that place.Are you curious to know?"

"Obvio," Anika replied.

"My plan is to walk a little more, and make some more use of my torch to investigate some real stuff in this wretched looking place."

"So, in other words, you mean to say that your plan is to just keep on walking until we are dead tired, and are completely bored and fed up with this mission. Am I correct?"

"Why to think so negative? Maybe we *will* find something."

"Is there any guarantee that we will find something worthy?" Anika asked, not liking the plan very much.

"Do you have any better plan?" Siya asked, expressionless. There was no answer for this question, Anika knew that. So she just followed Siya, wondering if the brownish dark colour of the ground and the rough walls would ever change.

They walked for about twenty minutes, sometimes silent, sometimes murmuring to themselves, sometimes asking if the other could see anything interesting or if could find a clue, sometimes dashing after any silver or green spot that caught their eye, only to find that the spot was just a drop or two of water, if silver or white and moss, if green.

After a while, the place again brightened up, as bright as the sun. In just a fraction of seconds, it seemed as if they had entered another world. They had come back to the glowing hemispherical ball, whose radiance had grown double within their last round. But this time, the radiations were not excruciatingly painful or blinding as the last time. The atmosphere seemed to be cheerful. The cardboard like thick paper had rolled itself, and swaying comfortably above the two hemispheres, as if sleeping happily.

"Should we go check what else is there inside that sliced sphere?" asked Siya.

"I would really love to know, but do you think it's safe to check?" asked Anika.

"It's worth a risk." Saying so, Siya advanced towards the sphere, which seemed to get bigger and bigger as she approached it.

"**DON'T COME CLOSER**" a deep grave voice boomed out from the thick paper, which started expanding in size. Within thirty seconds, the fifteen centimetre piece of old paper had turned into a sheet as large as 1 m $\times$ 1.5 m, and as thick as three fat Oxford dictionaries. The voice was deeper than the gushing tides of an ocean on a full moon day. And the echo seemed to reverberate a thousand times from everywhere.

Siya and Anika just watched, shocked, and at the same time scared. After some time, Siya managed to utter in a small voice, "Um, sorry. We just…um…"

"*DON'T COME CLOSER. PLEASE. YOU WILL BURN YOURSELF.*" It was the same deep booming voice again. Siya obeyed, not daring to move any further. Then the parchment returned to its previous original size.

"*THANK YOU. I MUST SAY, IT'S SO NICE TO HEAR SOMEONE HUMAN FROM EARTH TALKING TO ME AFTER MILLIONS OF YEARS. WELL, HULLO! MY NAME IS UDGHOSHAK, THE ONE WHO ANNOUNCES. I'M GLAD TO KNOW THAT SOME ARE STILL THERE WHO BELIEVE IN MAGIC. IN THIS MODERN WORLD FILLED WITH SUPERSTITIONS ABOUT SCIENCE AND TECHNOLOGY, IT'S HARD TO BELIEVE THAT SOMEONE HAS FAITH IN THE TRUTH OF MAGIC.*"

"Science…a superstition?" thought Siya and Anika, and exchanged quiet glances.

"SO WHAT BRINGS YOU HERE, YOUNG LADIES?"

"The place, where the first sun rays fall, as you said in that poem earlier. You said we'll find something there. We want to find out that place."

"AH! MY DEAR LITTLE FOOLS! DON'T YOU REALIZE THAT YOU HAVE ALREADY REACHED YOUR DESTINATION? DO YOU THINK YOU ARE ABLE TO TALK TO ME JUST LIKE THAT, WITHOUT DOING ANYTHNG?OH YES, MAYBE YOU ARE NOT FAMILIAR WITH THE RULES AND REGULATIONS OF OUR WORLD. WELL, YOU WILL SOON GET TO KNOW ABOUT ALL THIS. BUT FOR NOW, I WANT YOU TO SEE ABOVE."

The girls did as instructed, confused about all these new things, and excited at the same time. Initially, they didn't make out much, and couldn't understand why they had been told to look above. But they soon figured out. "The sunlight!" Both exclaimed at the same time, ecstatic with joy about their success. They started leaping and swinging madly. "So this tiny hole in the ceiling is the reason why the glow has brightened manifolds." Siya realized. "It allowed the sunlight to enter."

"CALM DOWN, GIRLS! CALM DOWN. YOUR MISSION HAS JUST STARTED NOW. YOU HAVE A LONG WAY TO GO. SIYA, YOU ARE NOT ANY ORDINARY GIRL. NEITHER ARE YOU ANIKA, JUST ANYONE CAN'T EARN THE TRUST AND FAITH OF SIYA. THIS SLICED SPHERE THAT YOU SEE, WITH IT'S TWO HALVES ROTATING IN JUST THE OPPOSITE DIRECTION HAS NOT OPENED SINCE AGES. MANY HAVE TRIED, BUT FAILED.

"DESTINY HAD CHOSEN SOMEONE GREAT FOR THIS TASK. NOW I DO NOT HAVE ANY DOUBT THAT THE GREAT SOUL IS NON OTHER THAN YOU. YOU WILL SOON COME TO KNOW THE PURPOSE FOR YOUR EXISTENCE. YOU WILL SOON UNDERSTAND WHAT'S YOUR MISSION IN THIS MAGICAL JOURNEY, AND I AM SURE YOU WILL BE SUCCESSFUL. I CAN SEE THAT ZEAL AND THAT DRIVING DETERMINATION GLAZING IN YOUR EYES. YOUR POWER IS EXTRA ORDINARY. EVERYONE DOES NOT HAVE THE CAPABILITY TO SEE AND REALIZE THE SPECIALITY OF THIS SPHERE WHEN IT'S LYING ON THE DARK FLOOR."

"But I do not possess any magical powers," Siya said, truthfully.

"POWERS ALWAYS NEED NOT BE MAGICAL. MAGIC LIES WITHIN ALL OF US. BUT VERY FEW OF US REALIZE IT'S POTENTIAL. SIYA AND ANIKA, THE PURENESS OF YOUR HEART, YOUR INNOCENCE, PATIENCE, WILLPOWER, BRAVERY, AND MOST IMPORTANTLY, YOUR HOPE THAT YOU WILL FIND IT OUT IS WHAT THAT DID THE MAGIC TODAY."

"But Udghoshak, what is that thing that you had told us to find in the place where the first sunshine falls?"

"OH YES! THAT THING! I HAD COMPLETELY FORGOTTEN ABOUT THAT. I WAS SO HAPPY FOR GETTING A CHANCE TO TALK WITH A GOOD EARTHIAN AFTER SO MANY DAYS. I AM SORRY, REALLY SORRY. THAT THING WHICH YOU WERE SUPPOSED TO FIND IS THIS STONE."

Udghoshak gave Siya a small copper sulphate coloured translucent stone.

"THIS WILL BE THE KEY TO YOUR SUCCESS," he said.

It didn't sparkle or had any visible beauty. It looked like any common piece of plastic, broken from a five-rupee ear ring. There was nothing spectacular in that stone, and yet there was a charming beauty in its simplicity.

After examining the blue vitriol coloured stone some more, Udghoshak handed down twelve ant sized diamond pieces to Anika.

"THE NEXT PUZZLE WILL BE MORE INTERESTING, BUT EASIER. YOU JUST HAVE TO MAKE A SHAPE WITH THESE DIAMONDS AND THE BLUESTONE. AND THE HINT THAT I GIVE WILL HELP YOU UNVEIL THE MYSTERY OF THE SHAPE THAT YOU HAVE TO MAKE."

"Okay, we are ready" Anika said, impatient for the next mystery that they were going to solve. "Just give us the puzzle!"

"BUT, BUT MY CHILD, THERE'S ONE THING THAT YOU'LL HAVE TO TAKE CARE OF." Udghoshak interrupted. **"YOU WILL NOT START MAKING ANY SHAPES UNTIL I TELL YOU TO DO SO, AND I SHALL NOT REPEAT THE HINT THIS TIME."**

"Agreed," Siya replied promptly.

"OKAY. SO THIS IS HOW IT GOES:

SOLVE IF YOU CAN

'I'M SOFT

I'M BEAUTIFUL

I'M LOVE

I'M GRACEFUL

I BLOOM

IN THE SUNLIGHT

I SHINE

IN THE MOONLIGHT

I SWAY

WHEN THE WIND BLOWS

I SMILE

WHEN THE SUN GLOWS

IF YOU ARE

A PASSER-BY

CAN YOU TELL

WHO AM I?'"

"Flower!" exclaimed the two girls happily, without taking an instant to solve the riddle, and at once settled down to make a flower shape with the diamonds.

"HAHAHA. THAT'S CORRECT. OKAY GIRLS, I HAVE TO LEAVE NOW. MY WORK IS DONE. JUST REMEMBER THAT THIS IS NOT SOME GAME YOU ARE PLAYING FOR FUN. JADOOI JAHAN, THE WORLD OF MAGIC, NEEDS YOU. I WILL AGAIN COME WHEN YOU WILL NEED ME. TATA ! I'M OFF!" Saying so, Udghoshak rolled himself. A pretty red-white loop appeared, which automatically tied itself around the roll, and prepared a neat knot around Udghoshak. The loop waved to the girls, with its one end, which appeared like a tiny hand while waving. Siya and Anika waved back to Udghoshak and the loop.

Within two minutes, artistic Anika had completed the flower design, using two diamonds for each of the six petals. Now, only the last touch was left, which Siya concluded by putting the bluestone right in the centre of the design.

"Pefect!" Anika cried out in delight. They kept watching it and admiring it for more two three minutes. Nothing happened. So they decided to wait for some more time. Still nothing happened.

"What's going to happen next?" Anika asked, not sure whether she was asking this to Siya or to herself.

"We don't know. Do you think this design will get transformed into a real flower or something?"

"And will it start talking to us, like it happened in *Alice in the Wonderland*?"

"Anything can happen. Let's not overburden our brain's power of imagination by thinking so much and just wait and watch."

They waited and waited and waited. And yet, nothing happened. Siya checked her cell phone for the time. The small hand was at seven, and the long hand at five. "We'll wait till seven fifteen."

"What do you mean by 'we will wait till seven fifteen'? Do we have any choice other than waiting."

"We will think what to do next."

They talked some more time on the 'if's and 'maybe's. Siya was half way through her sentence when Anika said, "Look!"

What they saw there was dangerous, for the ground had started cracking, and very soon it started shaking too. The centre of the cracks and vibrations was the flower's design which was trying to isolate itself from the ground. Siya and Anika distanced themselves from there.

"I'm afraid my eyes might come out from their sockets out of horror, like that of a snails," said Siya, quite frightened. By now, the rock beneath the flower shaped design had already taken the shape of the diamond flower, with the diamonds embedded on the rock. In not more than five seconds, the flower rock had started drilling like a screw driver into the earth's surface at a speed which seemed to be faster than the speed of light. Bits and pieces of all colours of rock went flying from the floor in all directions, as a result of the drilling. Anika backed away a little more. Siya became so curious of the scene being displayed in front of her that instead of coming backwards, she took a step forward to get a closer view.

The deeper the flower rock penetrated into the ground, the higher the bluestone soared, and the luminosity of the bluestone intensified all the more. While Siya was engrossed in the bluestone, a sharp red rock piece came flying towards Siya.

"Siya!" Anika screamed, terrified. Siya turned to face Anika, quite unaware of the danger driving towards her with racing speed. Then she saw it, and her eyes enlarged with terror. She shrieked, only the voice didn't come out; so afraid was she. Not knowing what to do, she closed her eyes and waited for the concequence.

MAYA

The red rock piece was just about to touch Siya, and Anika screeched "NO!" What happened next was utterly amazing. The rock piece hit Siya's forehead. And quite surprisingly for Anika, as soon as the red piece of rock touched Siya's soft temple, it transformed into a thousand red flowers.

Keeping her eyes squeezed, Siya asked, "Where am I? In hell or heaven? Should I open my eyes? Wait, do I even have my eyes now?"

"What are you muttering, idiot?" Anika asked.

"Who is speaking to me? Are you God? Are you Yamraj?"

"LOL Siya!" Anika said, laughing. "You are not dead. And I am Anika. Now, for heaven's sake, will you open your eyes?"

"Oh, I am alive! Anika, I am alive!" Siya was shouting. "I almost thought that red sabre would kill me. Oh! These flowers! Wow! Simply...simply beautiful! They look as red as fresh blood!"

"Do you know what happened? You closed your eyes...the red rock piece...the red flowers...it was so wonderful!" Anika started describing what she had seen, and their wonder was unimaginable.

"So what are you waiting for?" asked Siya. "Let's go!" In no time, the two girls were racing in circles around the flower shaped hole formed by the diamond-embedded flower rock, emitting millions and billions of all shapes and colours of flowers.

The bluestone, upon reaching its summit, became static; as still as a statue, and emitted sparkling silver-blue rays. Then the bluestone came down, and landed softly on Siya's palm, which she quickly tucked inside her skirt's right side pocket. In place of the bluestone remained its 3-D outline. The centre of the flower shaped hole radiated amber-pink beams of light, and junctioned with the silver blue rays. The two sets of rays started forming a link and bonded with each other in such a way that the final result was an enormous three dimensional diamond made of gleaming rays, enclosing a slowly spinning million year old book, yet as new-looking as a bud yet to blossom.

"I think this is what we needed to find." Siya declared.

"But how do we get that book? It's so high!" Anika said.

"Yeah, we will have to think of a way. Think, think, think."

"Thinking...we have to think...I hate to think. I really do," admitted Anika. "Think, think, think, think..."

"Thought!" Siya exclaimed happily.

"What? What have you thought of?" asked Anika eagerly.

"Let's tell that book politely to come down so that we can read it."

Anika cocked her left eye, "You'll talk with that book?"

"It's worth a try," Siya insisted.

"Wow! Awesome idea!" Anika clapped her hands sarcastically. "You think books talk? Have you ever heard a book talk in all your life?"

"Have you ever seen a piece of rock changing into flowers just by touching it?"

Anika remained silent. She knew Siya could shut anyone when she became logical, even if her logic wasn't always practical.

Siya went forward and spoke gravely, "O Great Book, please come down. We need you."

No response.

"See? I told you. Magic may exist, but it's not in our control." Anika gave her opinion.

"Please, Great Book. This is really necessary. Please, I pray you, please come down. Please!" Siya continued pleading, ignoring Anika.

"Please!" Siya cried out, bending on her knees, and her head held high with hope.

Silence.

"Oh please!" She prayed with all her heart, her eyes closed and hands joined.

Silence again.

Not finding any better clue, Anika also joined Siya. "Please listen to our prayers," she uttered softly.

Again silence.

"Why do you need the book?" The deafening stillness was broken by a melodious female voice, a tone as sweet as that of a nightingale. The source of the voice was a moving image of a pair of eyes, it's stare as deep as an ocean, a nose, and lips as attractive as a rose, but no face.

Siya raised her eyes, and fixed her gaze straight at the woman's eyes, and spoke honestly, "I do not know."

"If you do not know the necessity of this book, then how do you think that you deserve it?"

"The reason why I came here is solely curiosity, to know the secret of this place; but the purpose for which I want to have this book is because Udghoshak told us that your world, Jadooi Jahan needs us."

"Jadooi Jahan needs you? What do you mean? Why would our world of magic need a human? You must be lying. You must be a spy of The God of Demons. His plan of sending you through this entrance and not directly through The Great Black is very clever, but I am not going to be fooled so easily. No wonder the type of creatures he's been petting are strange...and now he has started keeping humans as well. There's no doubt that you are invaders. So return back and tell your Lord that he can't invade Jadooi Jahan as long as Maya's eyes are open and alive. I, Maya, the protector of this pious world of magic, swear this in the name of the Great Queen of Magic, the Queen of the most important empire, Jadooi Jahan's Mahashakti Rajeshwari!" Her words came out angry as red fire.

"But Udghoshak himself –

"Shut up! Not a word more about that idiot Udghoshak." Anika had just started her sentence, but unfortunately couldn't even complete a phrase.

"Last time an Asuri sneaked into the central Vatika...She blew the sleeping essence in the air... stole the Pavitra Pushpa and easily ran away! ... All because of the foolishness and innocence of Udghoshak! Additionally, if you should have been let in by any chance, then Udghoshak would have certainly informed me, and I should have got the entry application with The Queen's Mohar on it. Now I have no doubt that you are pure Asuris. GET LOST! NOW!"

"I don't get a word of what you are talking, but you are really making a mistake in identifying us," said Siya politely.

"Leave the kingdom of goodness and integrity. I shall not let your innocent talk fool me. I am not Udghoshak. Go away, you cruel Asuris! I said, GO AWAY! Open your wings and fly away this very moment, because if you don't do so, then –

"Then?" It was Siya. "Then what?" Siya said clenching her fists, thinking whether she was angry or afraid, because for some reason she really wanted to go to this place called Jadooi Jahan and see what was there and why Udghoshak had said that she was needed there.

"Then you'll regret it." The voice had the same sweetness, but was as cold as ice.

"Listen Maya, I don't know why I am here, or what I am doing here," said Siya. "But one thing I am sure of is that there's a kind of strange but strong urge inside me which is pushing me and compelling me to know the secret of this place, the secret that has remained hidden in my house since ages. Maybe I should simply forget about all this secret crap, and just let go of it. But there's some unknown driving force that even the thought of the secret of our mysterious storeroom kept me wide awake till late night every day."

"Enough of stories! Your cooked up tales are not going to feed me, Asuri kid! I'm giving you your last chance. Fly away!"

Siya did not move a centimetre. Anika panicked, thinking which would be a better option, suffering the result of provoking Maya's fury or to betray her best friend at the time when she should have been there with her to support her. Anika was deeply meditating on what would be the right choice, when Maya's blue-black eyeballs turned into bright orangish red and emanated flames of blazing red fire, that travelled straight through Siya, and to her great surprise, she remained quite unaffected, but it entered into Anika. "Aaah...Aaaaaaaaaaaaah!" cried Anika, now a body of burning bright orange cried in pain and agony. "Anikaaaaaaaaaaaaa!" Siya cried in horror.

THE HEALING POND

Siya rushed to hold Anika, who had fainted and had revived the colour of her body. The fire had died by now.

"Anika! Oh Anika!" Siya's eyes were swelling with tears. "Open your eyes. Speak to me! Anika!" Siya choked and cried bitterly.

Maya had lowered her eyes, filling guilty and disgusted with herself, for now she had correctly recognized who Siya was. ***"You... the agni didn't damage you! It can mean only one thing. It means...It means you are the one..."***

"What have you done to my friend?" Siya yelled at Maya, not listening to her. "Tell me! What have you done to Anika?" Siya shouted, tears streaking down her face. "What have you done to her?" She asked softly, sobbing.

"HULLO! I FORGOT TO TELL YOU, MAYA –

Maya raised her eyes to look at Udghoshak, and then looked down again, ashamed. She didn't even have the courage to apologize Siya and Anika, now that she knew who Siya Sharma was and what she had just done.

"OH MY GOD! ANIKA!" Udghoshak fretted for a minute at the sight of Anika lying unconscious in Siya's arms, but he soon realized the solution to it, and a tranquil calm replaced the worry on his pale brown-grey face. ***"DON'T WORRY SIYA, NOTHING HAS HAPPENED TO YOUR FRIEND. WE JUST HAVE TO TAKE HER TO THE HEALING POND."*** Udghoshak assured.

"FLYING FEATHER!" Udghoshak called out, and clapped his hands twice. And there came flying a pretty white feather, the size of a closed umbrella, and rested on Siya's palms. To her hands, it seemed as light as cotton. But when Udghoshak commanded ***"FLY,"*** the feather easily lifted her, as if she had no weight at all.

Within two minutes, they were hovering above a shimmering pond, shaped like a perfectly flat disk of metal, glowing golden under the slowly rising sun. The glorious sun was filling the sky with brilliant colours of red and splashed the clouds with endless rays of pink. She let the soft amber glow of the sunrise pour through her fingers and onto her upturned face. No sound rang out from the shimmering emptiness of space around it, except the splashing of freckled trout, or some creatures like that, leaping for flies and thunking on the statue still surface of the serene lake. It was lined with trees of all colours and shapes, the species of trees completely unknown to an amazed and bewildered Siya. The yellowish-orange grass beneath her feet was gleaming with pearl-like dew drops.

Siya was not exactly the person to observe and admire nature, not until she had got the assignment to write a poem or article that had to be nature-based. But the scene in front of her and the surrounding all around her was just so astounding that she couldn't stop herself from getting obsessed in it.

She was woken up from her daydream by the ruffled voice of Udghoshak, "***AREN'T YOU COMING DOWN***

FROM THAT FEATHER? LOOK, I HAVE SPRINKLED THE POND'S HEALING WATER ON YOUR FRIEND'S LITTLE FACE. SHE WILL BE WAKING UP ANY MOMENT. IT WAS ALL ACTUALLY MY FAULT, YOU KNOW."

"Your fault?" asked Siya, as the milk white feather landed her safely on the ground, and flew away by curving its peak towards Siya, as if bowing to her in respect. "How could that be your fault?" Siya repeated her question.

"I SHOULD HAVE INFORMED HER IMMEDIATELY THAT YOU ARE NOT INVADERS OR SPIES, BUT IN FACT, YOU ARE THAT POWER WHICH JADOOI JAHAN WAS SEARCHING SINCE FOREVER. BUT I WAS SO EXCITED AT YOUR ARRIVAL THAT I SPED OFF AT ONCE TO THE QUEEN TO INFORM HER ABOUT EVERYTHING. BUT ALAS! SHE WAS IN SUCH A BAD MOOD THAT SHE DIDN'T WANT TO HEAR ANYTHING. SHE DIDN'T EVEN WANT TO KNOW WHO HAS COME TO MEET HER. AND JUST THEN I REALIZED THAT I HAD CAME AWAY FROM THE CAVE WITHOUT INFORMING MAYA. I RUSHED THERE AT ONCE. BUT WHEN I CAME, IT WAS TOO LATE. BUT THANKS TO THE HEALING POND, NOTHING CAN HAPPEN TO ANIKA."

"But Udghoshak, I didn't understand one thing here –

"ONE THING? YOU MUST BE KIDDING ME. I THOUGHT YOU DO NOT KNOW ALMOST ANYTHING ABOUT THIS JADOOI JAHAN."

"Well, yeah. I really seem to know nothing about this place. But one thing that I'm sure about this place is that, here things are magical, and it's quite different from our place in all aspects," remarked Siya. "But what I'm most curious to know at this moment is that, there inside the gloomy cave, the first sunshine had fallen much earlier, but here the sun is rising now, even if this pond is just a two-minute distance from the cave."

"OH! THAT THING YOU SEE ABOVE IS NO SUN. IT'S PRAKASH, THE SHINE OF THIS POND ZONE. EVERY ZONE HAS ITS OWN SHINE. A SHINE'S GLOW IS SUCH THAT, IT CAN LIGHT UP THE ENTIRE ZONE. LIKE THE SHINE OF MADHUVAN IS MADHUCHANDRIKA, AND THAT OF SUSHOVIT VATIKA IS SWARNA. DRASHTA'S SHINE IS DIVYAJYOTI."

"There's a boy of that name in our school," Siya thought.

"THE GREATEST AND BRIGHTEST SHINE IS PRESENT IN THE SHAKTISTUPA – THE AMARSHIKHA."

Siya carefully listened to all the words that Udghoshak said, trying to digest all the new facts.

"AND BY THE WAY, I FORGOT TO TELL YOU, THE BOOK THAT YOU SAW IN MAYAMAHAL...

On looking at Siya's blank face, he added –

...MAYAMAHAL, THE PLACE WHERE YOU SAW MAYA, THE ENTRANCE TO JADOOI JAHAN... GETTING THE BOOK THAT YOU SAW THERE WAS NOT A PART OF YOUR MISSION AT THAT MOMENT, YOUR TEST WAS TO MAKE MAYA APPEAR IN FRONT OF YOU...AND YOU WERE SUCCESSFUL TOO. BUT I MADE YOU FAIL, COULD NOT GET THERE IN TIME...

"It's okay, Udghoshak," said Siya. "You know it's not your fault. What I want you to do right now is to throw some light on some more things that I don't know about Jadooi Jahan."

"OKAY. I WILL GIFT YOU SOMETHING THAT WILL HELP YOU KNOW SOME BASIC THINGS ABOUT OUR LAND."

Udghoshak closed his eyes and mumbled something, as if chanting a mantra, and there appeared a small CD sized book right in front of Siya's face, swaying in the air.

"THIS IS WHAT WE CALL AN ITTILA. IT'S A KIND OF ...WHAT DO YOU SAY IT IN YOUR PLANET...YES! IT'S KIND OF A DICTIONARY. YOU JUST HAVE TO SAY 'TURN' TO INSTRUCT THE BOOK TO FLIP ITS PAGES. TRY IT."

"Really? Okay. Turn!" And at just one instruction, the book opened, and in front of Siya's eyes was the picture of the most beautiful woman she had ever laid her eyes upon, in a long white gown embroidered with what looked like the world's costliest diamonds, her head crowned with a tiara which seemed more royal than Queen Elizabeth's. But what attracted her the most was her brown eyes. She felt strangely related to the figure that she was seeing, a kind of strong relative feeling that she herself could not define. The only word that came to Siya's mind on looking at this stunning picture was 'gorgeous'.

It was only after a whole two and a half minutes of surveying of every single detail of this picture that her glance fell upon the text below. Beneath the photo that seemed to have been snapped by the world's best photographer and photo editor, was written in bold letters-

MAHASHAKTI RAJESHWARI

The Great Queen of Jadooi Jahan

Finally feeling contended with the page, she instructed, "turn," and very obediently, the Ittila flipped to the next page – page 1. The initial letter of all the words on this page was A. It read –

Adwaita: The only hill in the world that sings

Agnidhara: river of fire

Alok: the shine of Agnidhara

Amruta: the sacred water of the healing pond

Anamika: a species of herb which hates to be called by any name or to hear any word that is said to address her (It springs itself on any person who dares to call it something and injures the person badly.) Anamika is the only word that the grass responds to and doesn't hurt the speaker.

Arpita: a special tree, also known as The Great Giver, which can offer a lot of things to a person in need (provided that the person is truthful, and deserves what he is asking for.)

Apsara: the winged pixies of Jadooi Jahan

Anish: the supreme figurine of magic

1

Siya had completed reading the first page and was just going to instruct the book to 'turn' to the next page when –

"Siya!" Anika awoke all of a sudden with a start.

"NOTHING" said Udghoshak comfortingly *"HAS HAPPENED TO YOUR BEST FRIEND, ANIKA. SO JUST CALM DOWN."*

"Is that true, Siya? Are you really alright?"

"Yeah, yeah. I'm totally fine," said Siya, leaving the Ittila floating in the air.

"That face, that witch who claimed herself to be the protector (adding extra drama to her voice and actions while saying 'the protector') of this Jazz...Jan... whatever this place is called –

"JADOOI JAHAN" Udghoshak corrected, which Anika, as expected, ignored.

"She was literally trying to attack you! To kill you! For one split second, I thought that I saw the horrible red fire-type thing get inside you, and then something hit me, and everything became a blur and –

"AND YOU WERE SEVENEERED"

"Seveneered?" Both of them asked at the same time.

"SEVENEERING IS A KIND OF SPELL WHERE THE VICTIM GETS A SUDDEN ATTACK AND FAINTS. BUT THEN ANIKA WAS DESEVENEERED, SO THERE IS NO QUESTION OF WORRYING."

"What is deseveneering?" asked Siya.

"DESEVENEERING REFERS TO THE SETTLING OF A PROTECTIVE LAYER ON A WEAK INNOCENT, WHEN A POWERFUL SPELL IS THROWN ON SOMEONE. AND SO, ANIKA WAS NOT HARMED."

"Are you sure that that bodyless woman was harmless?" Anika asked.

"OF COURSE. OF COURSE, MY GIRL," said Udghoshak. *"SHE IS REALLY GUILTY, AND FEELS SORRY FOR ALL THAT. IN FACT, SHE WANTED TO*

APOLOGISE YOU, BUT SHE FELT SO BAD THAT SHE DID NOT DARE TO SPEAK TO YOU."

"Oh" said Anika.

"WELL, I HAVE GOT TO GO AND INFORM THE QUEEN ABOUT YOU. LAST TIME I WENT TO HER ROOM, HER GUARD STOPPED ME AS SHE WAS REALLY UPSET ABOUT SOMETHING, AND DID NOT WANT TO HEAR ANYONE. SO OFF I GO."

"Wait Udghoshak," said Siya. "Before you go, I just wanted to tell you that please don't take too long to come. I need to get back to home by evening. If my mom gets to know that I had opened the store room, she would be mad at me."

"DON'T WORRY ABOUT THAT. YOUR WORLD AND OUR WORLD ARE QUIET DIFFERENT IN MORE THAN ONE WAY. IN OUR JADOOI JAHAN, IN FACT, IN THE WHOLE MAGICAL WORLD, YOU DON'T FEEL HUNGRY, YOU DON'T FEEL THIRSTY. IN JADOOI JAHAN, THERE'S NO DARKNESS, NO NIGHT AT ALL. BECAUSE OUR SHINES GLOW THROUGHOUT THE DAY, TWENTY FOUR × SEVEN. AND THE TIMES ARE ENTIRELY DIFFERENT FROM YOUR CLOCKS AND CALENDERS. ONE DAY ON YOUR LAND IS EQUAL TO ONE HUNDRED DAYS IN JADOOI JAHAN. AFTER ONE HUNDRED YEARS IN JADOOI JAHAN, YOU HUMANS SAY THAT ONE YEAR HAS PASSED. WHEN A CHILD IS BORN IN THIS MAGICAL WORLD, WE SAY THAT HE OR SHE IS ONE YEAR OLD AFTER ONE HUNDRED YEARS."

"Ohh...okay. I see."

"WELL SIYA, YOU SAID YOUR MOTHER DID NOT WANT YOU TO ENTER THE STOREROOM. THEN HOW DID YOU MANAGE TO GET INO IT?"

"Actually," she gave a toothy mischievous smile and said, "My parents have gone to my Grandma's home, as she is unwell. So I thought of sneaking into the room, as I really wanted to know it's secret. I wanted to know why my mom put such a severe restriction to that storeroom."

"HMM. SO THAT'S HOW YOU REACHED HERE. OH GOD, I AM AGAIN CHATTING. I HAVE TO GO AT ONCE," said Udghoshak hurriedly. *"SO GIRLS, PLEASE STAY HERE UNTIL I RETURN. IT'S VERY SAFE HERE. DON'T GO INVESTIGATING THE NEW WORLD ON YOUR OWN, OR YOU MIGHT CALL TROUBLE FOR YOURSELF. BYE!"*

Giving them a cheerful smile, Udghoshak rolled himself and disappeared.

"I'm sure the visit to this place is going to be the best of my lifetime." Anika squealed with joy. "Just as beautiful this pond is, I'm sure the whole kingdom would be marvellous too. We'd see magic, we'd fly high in the sky, we'd enter a real grand palace for the first time ever. Um..Siya…Siya! Siya!" Anika called out, surprised at her sudden absence. "Siya! Oh, so there you are. Why are you hiding behind the bush?"

"Shh" Siya shushed Anika and pulled her to her beside, gesturing her to keep quiet by keeping her index finger on her lips. "Look there."

"Where?" Anika asked in a confused whisper.

"There," said Siya "near the pond, behind that golden bush. Can't you see it moving?"

"Sure I can. But what's so surprising about it?" said Anika, looking at Siya as if she had gone crazy.

"Don't you see it? There's a hand behind it!"

"I can't see anything, Siya. I suppose you need an eye check up."

"It was just there now. Where did it go?" moaned Siya in despair. "Plus, I have a six by six vision. There's no question at all about my eyesight."

"Fine, fine. Maybe it's just another magical natural phenomenon of this world. After all, this place is all about magic, isn't it?"

"That's so creepy. But yeah, maybe you are right. Maybe it's just a *'magical natural phenomenon'* ," agreed Siya in unison, double quoating the words with her fingers, though she was still not satisfied with Anika's logic and couldn't stop thinking about what was there behind that bush.

"Now, come on Siya. Don't put yourself into worry for such a silly thing," Anika insisted.

"You're right. Maybe I'm just worrying my head off for nothing at all."

"I'm really looking forward for Udghoshak to return."

"Me too. But until he returns, let's just sit there near the pond and talk until he returns."

Anika liked the idea and quickly went with Siya to the pond edge to bask herself under the soft rays of Prakash. The sky was neither too bright, nor too dim; the air neither too hot nor too cold. In short, the weather was just perfect.

"I can't wait to explore all the new things," said Anika. "It's going to be so very exciting! It would be so much of fun, isn't it?"

"I bet, it would be awesome," said Siya, splashing the crystal clear pond water with her swinging legs.

"I wonder what type of organisms might exist here," said Anika, observing a green half fish-half bird popping its head out of the water and going back as quickly as it appeared, and reappearing again with a purple colour. "Would they be weird like the many in harry potter, or will they be beautiful like unicorns and mermaids, as in fairy tales?"

"I am most eager about Queen Rajeshwari. Look at this. This is an Ittila, a dictionary sort of thing."

Siya instructed, "turn!," and again the-all-obedient Ittila, which had gone to rest on the ground on seeing that nobody was paying attention to it for too long, flung to position in front of Siya and Anika, and dutifully opened to show them the gorgeous picture of Mahashakti Rajeshwari.

"Queen Rajeshwari" said Siya, "or as they say it here- Mahashakti Rajeshwari."

"How did you know that the queen is called Mahashakti here?" Anika asked casually, though not curious at this moment, as she was too busy imagining the type of creatures possible in Jadooi Jahan.

"It's written here in plain English, idiot. Plus, Udghoshak also told me" replied Siya, "when you had fainted. Do you think I will get a chance to meet the queen? Will I get the permission?"

ASSEMBLY

"You certainly should have the permission," said the melodious voice of a woman in a pearl-white flowing gown, more beautiful than the earth's fairest flowers, her face a reflection of moonlike glow, and her eyes glazing with fierce radiance. "I have full faith on you, general. But I must insist that we wait for some more time."

"But how long do we wait, your highness? How long?" asked a man with a square face, and a long black moustache, look of worry and anger on his face. "Danav commits regular murders, and we never do anything about it. Within this one week, Danav has already killed five pixies, stolen Pavitra Pushpa, and now he sends us the head of an innocent Lisam, whom he has beheaded as cruelly as possible. If this goes on, your highness, the day is not far when all the Lisams and pixies of Jadooi Jahan would be left dead and powerless under the feet of Danav. And as if doing all this was not enough, he has also sent us a warning message. And just in case you did not listen to it properly the last time, I …

The two pixies standing as guard in grey coloured frocks on either sides of Mahashakti Rajeshwari listened in terror, as the General marched to the royal notice-reader and snatched the parchment from his hand, containing Danav's message.

...would like to repeat the message to you -

Dear Mahashakti Rajeshwari,

First of all, how are you doing?

I did not have any intentions to disturb you, your highness, but I felt so sorry for the death of one of your Lisams that I could not stop myself from sending you a message. You see, I am so kind. I do not want to hurt you and your population (or should I say- just as you call all your helpless population of Lisams and coward pixies- your family). Because if you don't, then I will not be kind anymore to kill just one or two louts. I will finish off your entire kind. I shall destroy your family.

But as I am so very kind, I will not do any harm to anyone, if only you do me a simple favour. You just have to leave your throne to the one who deserves it, and that is me. I know you will be sensible enough to take the right choice as soon as possible. I am giving you a last chance to correct your mistake. I hope you understand the depth of your situation. Because if you don't, I assure you that you shall regret it.

P.S. I know that you will not do any foolishness to try to harm me. You are a sensible child.

Yours only

King of Andheri Jahan, Danav

Rajeshwari felt herself going red with anger, her fists tightened. But she knew that it was yet not the time to attack, and calmed herself.

"Do you still think, your highness, that he should go on doing crimes, and we should just keep watching?"

"Certainly not," said Rajeshwari. "We should do something. We must do something. But as I have already told you, General, the right time has not come. We will have to wait."

"But when will the right time come? Till when do we wait? And what are we waiting for?" This one question made Rajeshwari freeze, but she didn't show it. After all, who would understand who she was waiting for? "If Danav wants the throne" the General went on, "he will have to fight for it. Just give me one chance to battle against him, your highness, and we shall shred our sweat and blood to fight him. I will cut his throat and bring his head here at your feet," said the General, determined.

"I know Jadoooi Jahan has the best of the soldiers and rakshaks of the world. But I do not want them to sacrifice their lives for such a cruel and heartless monster."

"I understand your concern for the rakshaks and the soldiers, your highness, but dying proudly for their motherland would be much better than being killed like a coward," the General protested.

"General, please don't make my blood boil anymore in anger towards Danav's deeds. I don't want to lose my mind and get angry, which will make me take a wrong step," Rajeshwari said in a voice, which made the decision final. Then suddenly, she became emotional. "This very Shakti Bhawan was the place where I had sworn not to lose hope, not to lose patience. You know what Danav is capable of, don't you General? Do you think cutting his throat will put everything right? No, general. It won't. We are all aware of how powerful he is. You may kill him with your sword, but you would not be able to finish him off. He will again rise, more heartless and more monsterly than before, and then he would not just want this throne, but also want to rule the whole universe. We need someone who has powers to not just kill him, but… but…

"Five years, Eight years, Ten years, Fifteen years, however much time it takes…just wait." She heard this ringing inside her brain for the umpteenth time in her life. Flashes of that horrible day rushed through her mind, as it always did whenever she heard about Danav. The flashes that kept troubling her every day and every night, the flashes that kept her hope alive all these thirteen hundred years. "We just have to wait, okay?" She said, clearing her throat. "Assembly ends," she declared, as she rose from the Sinhasan where she was sitting. As a ritual, all other Lisam ministers and clerics rose from their seats and bowed to the Mahashakti, as she left the Assembly Hall in displeasure.

Everyone knew how much Mahashakti Rajeshwari hated the demon god –Danav, but no one knew what kept her from attacking him, and no one knew what she was waiting for all these years.

Rajeshwari headed up the stairs, straight towards her room.

"Don't allow anyone to come in." She ordered the two grey-frocked pixies, each flying from the left end of the door to the right end, and bumping into each other and irritably rubbing their head every now and then.

"Yes, your highness," said both the pixies at the same time, more like a song, and bowed to the Mahashakti.

Rajeshwari went inside and was just going to lock it from inside, when someone knocked on it.

"You are not allowed inside," said the pixie at the left.

"YOU SHUT UP AND MIND YOUR JOB," said Udghoshak coolly.

"It's the Queen's order," retorted the pixie at the right.

"MAY I COME IN?" asked Udghoshak, pushing the door ajar. **"YOUR HIGHNESS?"** he added.

"Come in Udghoshak," said Rajeshwari, pulling him in, and closed the door. "Now what is this stupid new way of teasing me by calling 'your highness'?" She asked irritably as she flung into the comfy majestic bed, more like a child than a queen. "You will always call me Rani, just the way you did when I was five, fifteen, and now when I am 25, and also when I become 85."

"OKAY, OKAY, MY RANI. FOR THE FIRST TIME IN SO MANY DAYS, I HAVE COME TO GIVE YOU SOME AWESOME NEWS!"

"Really?" asked Rajeshwari and crawled towards Udghoshak. "What?"

"I WON'T TELL. I WON'T TELL" said Udghoshak in a sing-song voice. **"YOU HAVE TO GUESS! THREE GUESSES!"**

"Why should I guess? You tell me," protested Rajeshwari.

"I WON'T TELL. I WON'T TELL" sang Udghoshak again in the same sing-song voice.

"Okay...Let's think...umm...The Pavitra Pushpa's location has been found out?" asked Rajeshwari, cocking her eyebrows.

"NOT YET. YOUR FIRST CHANCE IS OVER. SECOND GUESS?"

"Okay. Then it must be some festival, with some really good preparations.," said Rajeshwari, this time without much thinking. "Is there any occasion around the corner?"

"NO, NO, MY DEAR. GUESS SOME MORE."

"What else can it be?" said Rajeshwari defeatedly, now bored with the game.

"WELL. WELL. SEEMS LIKE YOU ARE EXHAUSTED WITH THE GUESSING GAME. SO ARE YOU READY FOR THE GRAND GREAT ANNOUNCEMENT?" said Udghoshak, chucking Rajeshwari's third chance, aware that he had left Siya and Anika waiting in the outskirts of the kingdom near the healing pond, and he must quickly get the Mahashakti's permission (as a formality) to bring the girls inside Jadooi Jahan.

"Yes, I am," said an enthusiastic Rajeshwari. "Please tell me quickly. Thanks God you didn't insist me to make a go for the third guess, or else I would have taken ages to guess something. Now, please tell me quickly what you are upto. What's the big news?"

"IT'S THAT FOR WHICH YOU HAVE BEEN WAITING SINCE THIRTEEN HUNDRED YEARS," said Udghoshak.

"Don't lose hope. Five years, Eight years, Ten years, Fifteen years, however much time it takes…just wait." The words rushed in her mind. Flashes of that day dashed in front of her eyes, as if she was again back in the day, right in the Shakti Bhawan… a vulnerable twelve year old, watching helplessly as everything got destroyed right in front of her eyes, and she just stood and watched.

"The messiah…" she gasped with a little smile turning up on her face. But the smile disappeared from her face as soon as it had appeared, and got replaced with a look of hopelessness. "No, it can't be –

"YES, IT IS," announced Udghoshak with a triumphant grin. ***"IT IS TRUE, RANI. YOU WERE RIGHT! YOUR FAITH FOR JADOOI JAHAN IS UNIMAGINABLE. YOUR HOPE AND PATIENCE HAS NOT GONE IN WASTE."***

"W..wh..wh…at …what do you mean?" Rajeshwari asked, as Udghoshak saw a glorious smile spread across her face after uncountable days. "You mean…you really mean…the Messiah has arrived?"

"YES! THE MESSIAH HAS ARRIVED, WAITING FOR YOUR PERMISSION NEAR THE BORDER OF JADOOI JAHAN, ALONG THE BANK OF THE HEALING POND."

"Well then what are we waiting for? Let's hurry and get them! And most importantly, let's announce this happy news to the lisams and rakshaks and pixies of Jadooi Jahan, let them celebrate in the name of the messiah, let's–

"NOT YET, RANI," said Udghoshak rigidly as he stopped Rajeshwari running down the corridors of the castle. ***"NOT NOW. EVERYONE IN JADOOI JAHAN DOES NOT KNOW WHAT HAPPENED ON THE NINETY NINTH DAY OF 15TH OCTOBER, 1999. AND MOREOVER, MAJORITY OF THE CITIZENS OF JADOOI JAHAN, ESPECIALLY THE LISAMS WOULD NEVER ACCEPT THAT OUR PROTECTOR IS A HUMAN."***

"A human?" enquired Rajeshwari, as if she had not heard correctly, a mixture of expressions of hesitation and amazement and shock spreading across her face. "Our messiah…a human?"

"YES, A HUMAN, A HUMAN GIRL, BUT A VERY DIFFERENT ONE FROM WHAT WE HAVE THOUGHT OF HUMANS TILL TODAY."

"But are you sure that the person whom you have found is really our messiah? I mean, the girl is not a lisam, not a pixie, not a rakshak also, not even someone from around Jadooi Jahan. It means that the girl is not even partially magical, she comes from somewhere far away from the reaches of the magical world, I still don't believe that she is the messiah. No Udghoshak, don't look at me like that. I am not disbelieving you, but I still can't see through it. How is a powerless, a magicless, a common girl from earth supposed to free us from the violence of Danav?"

"YOU DON'T UNDERSTAND THIS, BECAUSE YOU HAVE NOT SEEN HER. ONCE YOU LOOK INTO HER EYES, YOU WILL REALIZE EVERYTHING. THAT GIRL HAS GOT POWERS WHICH EVEN THE BEST OF JADOOI JAHAN'S MAGICAL CREATURES HAVEN'T."

"If you're so sure, then I guess –

"DO NOT WASTE ANOTHER MOMENT. NOW, HURRY UP TO THE HEALING POND. HER NAME IS SIYA, THIRTEEN YEARS OLD. SHE HAS A FRIEND TOO, ABOUT THE SAME AGE. HER NAME IS ANIKA. AND –

"Wait, why are you telling me all this?" asked Rajeshwari. "Are you not coming with me to pick them?"

"I WOULD HAVE LOVED TO WELCOME THEM INTO OUR WORLD, RANI. BUT YOU WILL HAVE TO GO THERE ALONE. I THINK I SHOULD RATHER STAY –

"All they need to enter Jadooi Jahan is just this," said Rajeshwari, and two double whorled flowers appeared in front of them, each with light pink coloured petals on the above, and the dark purple petals constituting the lower corolla.

"Here," she said, as she touched both the flowers, and the pink and purple pigments of the petals got transformed into transparent, and their edges started glowing splendidly. "This is all they need as a symbol to enter Shakti Bhawan's gates, right? They're ready now," she affirmed, as she progressed to hand them over to Udghoshak. "Then why should you not come along with me to the healing pond? What else do we need?"

"THERE'S A LOT MORE TO DO THAN JUST GIVING THEM THE PERMISSION AND ESCORTING THEM INTO THE CASTLE. MORE THAN HALF OF JADOOI JAHAN, PARTICULARLY THE HARDCORE LISAMS, AND ALL THE FRIENDLY NEIGHBOURING MAGICAL KINGDOMS WOULD NOT EASILY BELIEVE THAT A HUMAN IS OUR PROTECTOR. WE'LL HAVE TO MAKE THEM APPEAR THROUGH A NUMBER OF TESTS TO ASSERT THE CITIZENS OF JADOOI JAHAN THAT SIYA REALLY IS OUR MESSIAH. AND I WILL HAVE TO MAKE ARRANGEMENTS FOR ALL THESE TESTS OF PROOF. I WOULD ALSO NEED TO ARRANGE ALL KINDS OF JADOOI TRAINING, THAT MIGHT HELP HER AND HER FRIEND TO USE AND GET ACQUAINTED WITH VARIOUS MAGICAL POWERS."

"Okay, okay, okay. So altogether, the gist of your story is that you, by any means, are not going to come, right?"

"PRECISELY, RANI. THESE WORKS ARE REALLY IMPORTANT. I HAVE TO GET THEM DONE AS SOON AS POSSIBLE."

"Yeah, I understand."

"THIS IS HOW," said Udghoshak **"OUR PRETTY HUMAN GIRLS LOOK. NOTHING LESS THAN ANGELS."** He pointed his finger to the air, where all of a sudden an ink pen emerged out of nowhere and quickly sketched the exact outline of both the girls' faces.

"This… must be Siya?" asked an awestruck Rajeshwari, guessing correctly, to which Udghoshak gave a cheerful nod. "She looks so much like…" Rajeshwari stopped halfway through her sentence, as tears of amazement and overwhelming emotions filled her eyes, which she blinked away abruptly.

"YES, SHE DOES," Udghoshak affirmed with a smile. **"NOW GO."** He nudged Rajeshwari. **"THEY ARE WAITING FOR YOU."** Udghoshak waved, as he saw Rajeshwari disappear into thin air.

ENCOUNTER WITH
THE QUEEN

"This Udghoshak is taking ages to come," said Anika impatiently, in a tone full of boredom and irritation. They had now retarded from sitting near the pond's bank and waggling their legs inside the pond water, and taken to loitering around the pond. "This is the thirty second time I am taking a round around this pond."

"Are you seriously counting the number of times we have revolved around the pond?" asked Siya, not taking her eyes away from the Ittila swaying in front of her face, which was also taking tours around the pond with Siya.

"What else work do I have?"

"Read the Ittila with me."

"Wow! So interesting!" Anika mocked in sarcasm.

"It is interesting, Anika. Reading about things which one could have only imagined earlier is definitely interesting."

"You are still imagining those, Siya. The magic is not really happening in front of you."

"You have a point there. And that's why I am telling you to read this," suggested Siya. "as all the contents of this book are soon going to gain life when we enter Jadooi Jahan, and the magic would be right in front of us."

"Yes. And that's why I want someone to come and take us to Jadooi Jahan, now that I have waited so long and taking the thirty third round around this pond, so that I can actually experience the real magical world, and not just imagine about it." Anika gave her logical explanation.

Seeing that Siya was not contempted with her logic, she added on, "Siya, I know that the book is interesting, but informative would be a better word for it. And I did enjoy reading it for the first fifteen -twenty minutes, but I can't just go on reading that book for an hour like you."

"Is someone waiting for me?" asked a melodious female voice from behind them. They turned back, and saw a figure that they were familiar with now.

"Mahashakti Rajeshwari!" Anika exclaimed, awestruck by the woman's beauty.

"So I am," returned the beautiful lady in front of them.

"Are you... are you really Mahashakti Rajeshwari? The Great Queen of Jadooi Jahan's empire?" asked Siya in unbelievable amazement.

"Any doubt?" asked The Queen.

"No, of course not," replied Anika instantly.

"What are we waiting for then? I must take you to your destination," said The Queen, with particular emphasis to Siya. "Are you not eager to talk with the clouds, sing with the birds, and fly into Jadooi Jahan this very moment?" she asked as she bent towards Anika.

"Yes, I am," replied a madly excited Anika, who was almost jumping crazily with joy. "Very much, I am."

"Then we should not waste any more time. I will take you to Jadooi Jahan in the most magnificent ride that the magical world has ever known of. *Pawan!*" she said aloud, and closed her eyes. A huge swan-shaped vehicle appeared above them, and came down to the ground, vigorously flapping its wings. She opened her eyes and gestured Siya and Anika to get into it, and at once the swan vehicle soared to the sky with a swift speed, and the healing pond was soon out of the sight.

"Wow! Wo-o-o-w!" Anika was hopping like a frog from one side of the swan's wings to another. "This is simply fabulous, fantastic, amazing!"

"Yeah, there's no denying that." Siya piped in, enthralled by the mesmerizing view of Jadooi Jahan. From trees of all varieties of colours and shapes to beautiful extraordinary creatures were swinging and dancing, half of which they had only read in books, and the other half that they had never imagined in their dreams. They escalated high and high, until the magnificent buildings were just tiny specks, and the shines dangled below them like hanging candles.

"Queen Rajeshwari, I mean, Mahashakti Rajeshwari, can we fly a bit down if you don't mind?" requested Anika, trying to sound like the most polite person in the world. "So that we can get a closer look of the scenery?" She asked expectantly, but all she received as a reply was only silence.

Not satisfied with the unwelcoming response, she intentionally cleared her throat and asked, "Excuse me, Mahashakti? Could we please fly a bit down?.," this time in a deliberately raised voice.

"Yes? Did you ask me something, child?" asked The Queen plainly, as she flew the swan-shaped vehicle even more higher, giving Anika an impression that magical people were probably half-deaf, with the possible exception of Udghoshak.

Now they had come so high that Jadooi Jahan below them was only a blur, and above them was a small black dot, which seemed to get bigger and bigger like an emerging tornado, as and as they got nearer to it.

"Something is wrong," thought Siya tensely, as they were near to approach the black tornado like thing.

"Stop!" ordered Siya, in a commanding tone.

No answer. No response at all.

"I say, stop!" Siya commanded again.

"Who are you to stop me?" said a cold voice from the front, as they saw the beautiful white laced gown turn into a gorgeous bright green robe, which continued to elongate until it reached the faces of the terrified girls, who had now backed off to the extreme edge of the long swan vehicle, and the robe stopped extending after a final attempt to almost throw the girls out of the swan's lap.

"Mahashakti, that magic you showed us by changing the colour of your gown was really great!" said Anika, forcing a small laugh. "But maybe you can show us the magic in a slightly lower altitude? I think I have got a fear of heights. What do we call it Siya? Heightophobia?"

"HE HE he he ha ha HA HA" they heard the queen give a cold evil laugh. "I love the way you address me as Mahashakti, as I am soon going to be," she said snobbishly, as she turned to face Siya and Anika, with a heavy stamp on the floor that made her long green robe fly in the air for half a moment before settling on the floor of the vehicle, which had also undergone transformation from the pure white swan shape to what looked like a magnanimous dirty brown-black dragon, with large glinting malicious eyes and a tail as long as the dragon's body itself.

What they saw in front of them made their lower jaws drop, for what stood before them was not Mahashakti Rajeshwari, but a woman of twenty five or so with the most perfect figure: long skinny legs and a slim body covered in a forest green mermaid gown, a face just as beautiful as Mahashakti Rajeshwari's, with attractive blue eyes, stunning red lips, lovely white cheeks, long golden hair. But instead of the calm and peace that Siya had felt in Mahashakti Rajeshwari's look in the picture that she had seen in the Ittila, this woman's eyes revealed pride and superiority. And the way she curved her lips in an evil smirk was what made all her prettiness ugly in front of the charming smile of Mahashakti Rajeshwari. "What? Afraid, are you? You are afraid, aren't you?"

"HE he he he HA HA ha ha ha HA HA HA he he HA HA HA" she again laughed like a wild witch, the same haughty laugh, as if with even more pleasure. "I can't believe that a rat like you could be chosen as the *'messiah'*. Of course, this Jadooi Jahan is full of fools and louts, just like your friend Udghoshak who thought that only a Suraksha protective shield would keep you protected. Well, you don't even know the simplest arts of magic." She said, as she played with her wand, the size of a broomstick, with a skull at the top. She placed it in a wand-holder sort of thing and walked towards the girls, as the dragon drived into the tar black tornado.

Now all they could see around themselves was only darkness and darkness and darkness. Surprisingly, they could see each other very clearly, even in the midst of the pitch black darkness. "How could they think that someone like you could save them from the greatest conjurer of the world, someone who can't even save herself?" said the woman with supreme vanity, and went to stroke the vehicle's dragon head, as if it was her pet. She continued to blame Siya and Mahashakti Rajeshwari and the people of Jadooi Jahan as foolish, timid and coward, when Siya took the opportunity to tiptoe to the wand holder.

She had hardly touched the wand when something sharp incised into her skin, and her hand started bleeding. "Ahh!" she yelped, as something slithered over her. Pangs of pain rushed through her head, as she tried to see what had bit her. "It's not that easy to fool Naagin," hissed a voice in her ear, and before she could think of anything else, everything around her became a blur, and then vanished away.

NIGHTMARE

"Siya!" shrieked Mrs. Sharma, as she woke up with a start with sweat all over her face. This made Mr. Sharma jump out of the bed.

"What happened? Are you okay, Meera dear?"

"Siya…where is she? Where is my child?" asked Mrs. Sharma worriedly, wiping her face with her saree.

"Oh God! We are at your mother's home, Meera. Siya is sleeping soundly at home. She is alright. You also go back to sleep."

"But… you don't understand…she…she –

"Meera, it was just a bad dream. Now forget it, and go back to sleep," said Mr. Sharma, as he made his wife lie on the bed, and pulled the blanket over her. "Close your eyes, and sleep as much as you can in this afternoon. Because at night, you will have to be with Maa, as she would be awake at night because of these medicine doses," he said, and went back to sleep.

Mrs. Sharma lay in her bed with opened eyes, trying to remember what she had seen. But all that she could recall was a very dark place, and Siya telling "Ahh!" as she fell down in agony, and then it seemed as if the dark swallowed the darkness, and the next moment she had found herself all sweaty on a bed, with her husband trying to comfort her back to sleep. She tried hard to recollect what exactly had happened in the dream, but it was the same like trying to keep water from flowing from a pot full with holes. After several attempts, she decided to give rest to her tired brain, and fell into a dreamless sleep.

THE SEARCH

"Siya! Anika!" called Rajeshwari. "Siya! Siya! Can you hear me? Anika! Oh, where are you two? It's been two hours since I am searching these girls, and there's not a trace of either of them," retorted Rajeshwari. "I have looked for them in every nook and corner of this zone, and they are nowhere to be found. Is there any place that I have left out? Ah, yes. The golden bush!" She rushed towards the healing pond.

She progressed towards the golden bush, and started inspecting the place. Then finally, she spotted someone. But this someone was neither Siya, nor a girl. "Moreover, Udghoshak had told that there would be two human girls," thought Rajeshwari. "But this child lying here seems to be a human boy. And there's just one child here, not two. What does he think he is doing here? How did he come here, in the first place? Curse you, Udghoshak. You should have come with me. But pity you had other necessary works to do."

"Let's wake this boy," she decided. She gently stroked the boy's hair, and chanted something, and the boy lazily stirred up.

"Oh, when did I fall asleep?" muttered the boy under his breath. When he saw Rajeshwari, his eyes broadened, as if mesmerized, for in front of his eyes stood the most beautiful woman he had ever laid his eyes upon, in a long white gown embroidered with what looked like the world's costliest diamonds, her head crowned with a tiara which seemed more royal than Queen Elizabeth's. But what attracted him the most was her brown eyes. The only word that came to his mind on looking at this stunning lady was 'gorgeous'.

The soft strokes on his hair were no less than the caress of a mother. He felt as though he was dreaming about a fairy, and then he remembered that he was actually in a magical world, and not on earth.

Rajeshwari stopped fondling with his hair, now that she was determined that the boy was awake. "What are you doing here?" she asked straightly.

"I…I…uh…I…that…um…I…I…I…" the boy fumbled over his letters, as he searched for words to phrase a sentence. "I should ask that to myself," he thought. "What am I doing here?"

"I..um.." he tried again, but failed.

"Okay, it seems you are still drowsy. What is your name?" asked Rajeshwari.

"Abhilash," he gulped. "Abhilash Malhotra," replied the boy.

"You are, for sure, a human boy from earth, aren't you?" asked Rajeshwari.

"Yes," said Abhilash, not finding any other answer for this awkward question. "And who are you? An angel?" he asked.

"No. Of course not," Rajeshwari replied with a laugh. "Angels and fairies are only in books and stories. I'm a lisam."

"Never heard of that word," said Abhilash honestly.

"Not surprising," said Rajeshwari.

"What's your name?" asked Abhilash. "I mean, what should I call you?"

"My name is Rajeshwari. You can call me by whatever name you wish."

"Ra-je-shwa-ri. You have got such a long name!"

"People call me Mahashakti. So in short, you can call me MS."

"MS, that's cool. I will call you MS," said Abhilash, liking the short form. "Wait, I think I have heard this word Mahashakti...um...oh yes! Those two were saying that Mahashakti means..." and then his eyes broadened, as he looked at Rajeshwari with even more admiration and respect, "The Queen? You are the Queen?"

"Yeah, sort of," said Rajeshwari.

"So do I have to address you by saying 'your highness'?" asked Abhilash.

"No, that's not required," said Rajeshwari. "You liked the name MS, didn't you?"

"Am I allowed to call a queen like that?" asked Abhilash.

"Yes, if she herself allows you to. And I love to be addressed informally, as a very few people do that. Well, how did you come here?"

"I..arr...I actually," began Abhilash, thinking how to put it. "Well I shouldn't have done that...I..um...I followed Siya and Anika."

"Ohh"

"Where are they?" asked Abhilash.

"Good God! I was just going to ask you the same question," said Rajeshwari.

"Ohh"

"My goodness! I have been searching for the last two hours and ten minutes, but I still can't find them," Rajeshwari fretted. "I have scanned the entire zone for these girls; every tree, every bush, every grass. But they are nowhere. Where could have they gone?" said Rajeshwari in despair.

"But they were right there this morning, waggling their legs in the pond and taking rounds of that pond."

"Why were you following them, by the way?" Rajeshwari asked suspectively.

Rajeshwari again found Abhilash speechless, as a blush formed over his face.

"Why does she have to ask that?" thought Abhilash. "What does she expect me to tell? The truth? That I have kind of a crush on Siya, for which I grabbed the opportunity of her parents' absence and rushed to her house in midnight like a maniac by lying to my parents that I was going to attend Vikram's late night party? And that I had thought my plan of scaring her like a ghost with my magic candle and then saving her like a hero as a super dooper idea, until I came to her spooky store room and got the scare for my life myself?"

"Where are you lost, Mr.?" asked Rajeshwari, clicking her fingers in front of Abhilash's eyes. "Okay. Never mind. That's none of my business."

"Thankyou!" said Abhilash, relieved.

"Thank you?"

"I mean...never mind. Let's drop the topic," insisted Abhilash. "Should we try to find Siya and Anika? You said you had been trying to find them for quite a long time."

"That's true," said Rajeshwari. "But how do I find them?"

"Don't you have any magical device to track her or something? Even in our non magical earth, we can track the location of a person's mobile phone?" asked Abhilash smartly.

"Device? Track? Magical phone? What are you talking of? In case your planet's people speak some different language, please switch to English," said Rajeshwari.

"I guess your magical place knows very little of modern science and technology," said Abhilash with pride.

"Does science really exist? Isn't it only a superstition?" asked Rajeshwari curiously.

"Science, a superstition? Are you kidding me? The whole world is governed by scientific laws. Each and everything in this universe has a science behind it!"

"I would have said the same thing for magic," said Rajeshwari. "Our world and yours are so very different."

"I know, right?" agreed Abhilash. "Just a day ago, I would have thought that magic is a superstition."

"MAGIC AND SCIENCE ARE NOT TWO OPPOSITE THINGS. EVERY MAGIC HAS A SCIENCE BEHIND IT, AND EVERY SCIENCE BECOMES MAGICAL, ONCE IT'S UNDERSTOOD. AND FOR ACHIEVING THE GOAL, MAGIC AND SCIENCE WILL HAVE TO JOIN HANDS. APPARENTLY, OUR GOAL IS TO FIND SIYA AND ANIKA. AND AS MUCH AS THE INFORMATION

COLLECTED BY MY SPY INSTRUMENTS TELLS, WE ARE IN DEEP TROUBLE.*

"What has got stolen this time, Udghoshak?" asked Rajeshwari.

"OUR MOST INVALUABLE TREASURE, OUR LAST HOPE. DANAV HAS ABDUCTED SIYA AND ANIKA."

KIDNAPPED

Abhilash gasped in shock. Rajeshwari's fists tightened, her blood started boiling, her face was a storm of fury, her eyes almost red with rage. "I will not forgive him!" she swore.

"TAKING ADVANTAGE OF BEING A REPTILADY, NAAGIN USED HER SERPENTINE POWERS TO CONVERT HERSELF INTO YOUR FORM, RANI. AND THE GIRLS GOT BEFOOLED. THEY THOUGHT THAT IT WAS REALLY YOU WHO HAD COME TO PICK THEM UP TO JADOOI JAHAN."

"Who is Danav? Why did he kidnap them?" asked Abhilash.

"FIRST GIVE ME YOUR BOMILE," said Udghoshak urgently.

"Sorry?" asked a perplexed Abhilash.

"NOBILE PHONE YOU CALL IT, DON'T YOU?"

"Oh, you want my mobile." Abhilash looked in his left jeans pocket, where he found the magic candle that was supposed to burn and fuse, burn and fuse, and burn and fuse again, and according to his plan – along with his creepy equipments, he would have scared Siya. He then searched in his left pocket, only to find a handkerchief. Finally he found his cell phone in his shirt pocket, which was immediately grabbed by Udghoshak.

Udghoshak did some work on it, though he didn't touch the touch screen at all. *"HER NUMBER IS 7658434419, RIGHT?"*

"Yes," Abhilash nodded, who had Siya's number engraved in his mind, even though he had never called her.

"GOOD. JUST AS I TOLD YOU, MAGIC AND SCIENCE TOGETHER CAN BE OF GREAT HELP."

"What are you trying to do with that object?" asked Rajeshwari. "How can it help to save Siya and Anika?"

"I FOUND OUT SIYA'S CONTACT BY THE MAGIC OF WILL. THE CONTACT OPENED AT ONCE. NOW YOU TRY THE VISUAL MAGIC, I THINK IT MAY HELP."

"That's a great idea!" said Rajeshwari happily, and then closed her fists over the mobile phone and uttered "show your possessor". "Show your possessor. Show your possessor" she repeated. The mobile now beamed rays, and displayed Siya's face on the ground, as if it had all of a sudden got converted into a projector.

"IT WORKED!" exclaimed Udghoshak. Rajeshwari nodded gladly.

"Check the possessor's safety. Check the possessor's safety" said Rajeshwari, as if she was talking with the phone.

"Safe," hissed the phone. "No injuries."

"Thanks God," said Rajeshwari with relief. "Siya is alright. Now Anika. Do you have her contact as well, Abhilash?"

"I have the whole class's number." He beamed proudly.

"Very well. Then the will of magic should bring out her contact too," and quite surely, it did. "8647301966, am I correct?"

"I don't remember everyone's number. But if it's displaying Anika's name, then it must be."

"Yes, her name is there," said Rajeshwari. "Show the possessor," she said, and Anika's face was displayed on the ground, this time at only one command. "Wow! It worked again," she said with double joy of the success. "Check the possessor's safety. Check the possessor's safety."

But this time, there was no voice, no response at all. Rajeshwari pursed her lips tensely, and then tried again, "Check the possessor's safety. Check the possessor's safety."

Still nothing happened.

"IF SIYA IS SAFE, ANIKA SHOULD BE SAFE AS WELL," said Udghoshak.

"I hope so," said Rajeshwari. "I can't understand what's going to happen. Jadooi Jahan's throne's supreme power, the truthwand was taken by Danav. Then he stole the Pavitra Pushpa, the life giving flower, with which he has made a whole new army of Asuras and Asuris. And now, our last hope, Siya is also in his captive.

"He has added all the evil powers of his deathwand to the pureness and the potential of the truthwand, which in other words makes him the most powerful ruler of the entire magical world. In his terror, even our friendly neighbouring kingdoms have stopped giving us help and support. The only thing that he is waiting for is to create a greater unbeatable force of Asuras and Asuris. Once his demon army becomes huge and strong enough, nothing can stop him from taking over Jadooi Jahan. Even God won't be able to stop him from bringing destruction and doom in our lives."

"RANI, JUST CALM DOWN. DON'T MOVE FROM HERE TO THERE," advised Udghoshak to Rajeshwari, who was exactly doing the same, that is, moving from here to there and from there to here.

"Oh, so Danav is the villain of this story."

"FIDGETING WON'T HELP, RANI," said Udghoshak, not paying attention to what Abhilash was saying. **"JUST SIT DOWN. THERE MUST BE A WAY."**

Considering Udghoshak's suggestion, Rajeshwari went near the pond, and bent on her knees on the yellowish-orange grass. Abhilash and Udghoshak followed her and sat down. Rajeshwari had just started waving her hand in the water, creating round currents in the pond, when she jumped to her feet and announced, "I have an idea!"

"You say that just like Siya!" said Abhilash, surprised by the resemblance. "Every time when we get a group project work, she's always like- "I have an idea!"

"Ohh, great!" said Rajeshwari without enthusiasm. "Now listen to me. I think that the mind-to-mind connect charm can help us."

"HOW DOES THAT WORK?" asked Ughoshak. **"I HAVE NEVER LEARNT IT."**

"In this charm, with the help of amulets, two persons of the same variety can communicate with each other without speaking, provided that they are within a mile's distance."

"Can't I just call her?" asked Abhilash inquisitively. "It would be much more easier and simpler."

"You mean contact her? With that scientific object of yours?" asked Rajeshwari.

"Yes"

"THAT IS NOT POSSIBLE," said Udghoshak. ***"THERE IS NO OMBILE TOWER HERE."***

"Mobile tower," corrected Abhilash, irritated.

"Udghoshak, I believe you have given Siya a proper amulet?" asked Rajeshwari.

"I HAVE," Udghoshak said proudly. ***"I HAVE GIVEN HER THE BLUESTONE."***

"That was a good choice!" said Rajeshwari, impressed. "Then it sorts out our problem for the time being. We need two things in a mind-to-mind connect charm. As I have already told, one is two people of the same variety, and the second is two amulets with each. And thankfully we have a human with us. Abhilash, now only you can find Siya."

"YOU WILL HELP US, WON'T YOU?" asked Udghoshak.

"Of course, I will," said an affirmed Abhilash to Rajeshwari and Udghoshak in a 'leave-it-on-me' voice. "But what do I have to do?"

"Listen to me carefully," said Rajeshwari. "We will go to Andheri Jahan, the kingdom of Danav. You will be playing the main role, as only you can contact Siya's amulet, her bluestone. I will give you an amulet. Tell me your favourite colour."

"Transparent," answered Abhilash immediately.

"That's not a colour," said Rajeshwari with a smile. "But I can give you a transparent amulet."

She closed her eyes and raised both her hands to the air, her face upturned towards Prakash's glow. And there appeared in midair, a small polished transparent ball, the size of a table tennis ball, looking like a round bead.

"Show your hand," Rajeshwari instructed. "It's the crystal orb. Keep it with you always," she said, as the crystal orb flied to Abhilash and rested on his outstretched palm."

"Thankyou. It's beautiful," said Abhilash joyfully.

Rajeshwari gave a smile, and then continued, "If the person bearing the amulet is within one mile, then your amulet starts glowing. So in this case, if Siya is within a mile's reach to you, your crystal orb will start dazzling and glowing. The nearer you get to Siya, the brighter will be the orb's glow. Then what you have to do is to hold the crystal orb firmly in your right hand, remember- right hand, with the thumb above the other four fingers, and close your eyes. You won't have to concentrate very hard or anything, but you do have to be focused and calm. Once you do so, you will see a silhouette of Siya's figure. The silhouette is an indication that the other person's amulet has started glowing. I hope you understood everything?"

"Yes," said Abhilash. "I am ready. Let's go!"

"OKAY. LET'S GO" said Udghoshak.

"Flying Feather!" called out Rajeshwari, and two milk white feathers showed up. Udghoshak told Abhilash how to use the feather, and the three were soon flying in the sky, headed towards Andheri Jahan.

BETRAYAL

Siya woke up with a shudder, as she thought of the last words that she had heard in her dream. *"If you have courage, then fight with me like a true warrior."* Someone in a silk sky blue gown was saying, whose face Siya couldn't see, as she was seeing this lady from behind. Then someone else was laughing evilly and saying, *"A true warrior is one who has brains, and knows how to win the battle."* Then there was clank of metals, and thuds and thumps and sizzling sounds, and all Siya was seeing was just sharp beams of light flying from from one place to another. It could have been a laser show, but the atmosphere in her dream wasn't that of a festive mood. The last thing that she had heard was a loud painful shriek of a woman, and the next moment she had found herself on a shabby jute rug, wondering what she had just seen in her nightmare.

After she had done with rubbing her eyes and thinking a good bit about her dream, she suddenly realized that the place where she was lying right now was totally strange to her. What was this place, what was she doing here, she thought. And then it all came to her in a rush.

Of course, she was in Jadooi Jahan, the land of magic. And then Mahashakti Rajeshwari had escorted them to somewhere in a swan-shaped ride. Wait, was that woman really Mahashakti Rajeshwari? Surely, she wasn't. She had changed into another woman right before her eyes! This scruffy and dark room couldn't be Jadooi Jahan, right? What was this place then? How long had she been here? Where was Anika? And what was that venomous bite that she had got in her left hand?

All kinds of questions came dashing to her mind, as she rubbed her left hand. The pain had subsided, but not entirely. There were two tiny black spots on them, making it clear that only a snake could have done this damage.

"Anika!" she called slowly.

No response.

"Anika!" she called, a bit louder.

Yet no response.

"Anika, where are you? Anika!" now she started panicking, and shrieking at the top of her voice. "Anika, can't you hear me? Anika!" she cried out aloud. But all she could hear was only her voice booming in the silence.

"Anika! Where have you left me alone in this eerie dark room?" she called in a whisper, now sure that no one could hear her. She again tried to remember what had happened before she was asleep. But all she could recall was something slithery biting her, and a woman named Naagin hissing that defeating her was not easy.

Not able to get any clue of her present situation, she decided to make a survey of the room. It was an extremely gloomy room, but there was a candle thankfully, which gave the room a slight glow. The walls were all dark green. There was no window or skylight. There was a door which Siya couldn't open even after applying force on it for five whole minutes, and thus came to the conclusion that it was locked from outside. There was a small crack in the door, which revealed that the outside of the room was as black as coal. "Has someone locked me here? If so, then who? And why, why me?" She brought the candle to the crack on the door, and strained her eyes to see what was there beyond the door. But all that Siya could see was the same dark green floor and walls, like that of the room, and a staircase leading to somewhere which she didn't know. She tried to give a final hard hit to the door, which was to no effect. "Couldn't have expected the door to open with a bang, anyways," she thought, trying to be sarcastic to herself, which would keep her calm and out of stress and worry.

Unable to have any success in knowing her current position in the globe, she returned to her inside-the-room inspection and kept the candle in its place. There was a very dusty closet to her right corner. A broken lamp set stood slanted near it, like the leaning tower of Pisa, looking as if it might fall any moment. Except these four things; the shabby rug, the undusted closet, the lamp set, and the wonderful little candle, there was nothing else in the room (there was nothing wonderful about the candle, which Siya saw as just a white mound of wax, but when comparison had to be done with anything in this room, Siya didn't see anything else more cheerful than the small but bright flame of the candle.)

She shifted her attention to the closet, and made her mind to get a look at its components (which would most likely be of no interest to me, she thought). And quite expectedly, the wardrobe was opened by her only to reveal a thicker layer of dust on its top two shelves, and a comparatively thinner crust of dust on the lowermost shelf. The top shelf did not have anything except dust. The second shelf had a packet of candles, and a matchbox. The third shelf again had nothing. Nothing, other than a long piece of thread, which was obviously of no use to her, so that could just as well be counted as 'nothing'.

She investigated the room for about a quarter of hour, and then got bored and disgusted with the search and settled down on the tattered bed cover lying on the floor. She took out a kitkat chocolate from her skirt pocket, and started chewing it, even though she didn't feel hungry. Of course she couldn't be hungry here, as she was in the magical world. But as she anyways didn't have any other job, she continued chewing it, forgetting all other worries in the sweet taste of the kitkat.

She put her hand again in her pocket to get another chocolate, but what came out in her hand was a little copper sulphate stone, having no particular shape whatsoever.

"The bluestone," she uttered. She looked at it from all angles. "How had I never noticed this," she asked herself, as it now caught her eye that the stone had two small holes on each side of it. "Wow! I can wear this as a necklace." She got up and went to the closet again, and picked up the piece of thread from there.

"So you are not that useless after all," she told the thread. She spent the next ten minutes cutting and biting the thread to the right size, and pushing it through the hole by squinting her eyes. After giving a final knot to the thread, Siya was satisfied with her work and wore it. "Perfect!" she smiled, as she peered down to look at her self-made necklace. And suddenly, the cuts of the stone began glimmering. And a light flickered inside it, and then got fused.

"Did this just glow?" she thought. And a light flickered in it once again, but soon died. "Why was the bluestone glowing? I don't understand anything, what's exactly happening?" And as if to give her a clue, she heard faint voices coming from outside the room, which slowly got louder and louder, as the voices seemed to get nearer and nearer.

"Come with me, I've kept her here," said a melodious but cold female voice. "I have not killed her, though. I thought it best to take your permission first, before taking any action on Siya." Siya froze at the mention of her name, that too with the word 'kill' in the same sentence.

"That was a good decision, Naagin love. She's my prey, and only I will kill her," said an extremely shrill and a colder voice. "And I will kill her in front of Rajeshwari." The voice was growing more and more malevolent. "I still don't believe that she returned, Naagin. I thought humans didn't have magical powers."

"And you! Why should we believe that you are on our side, and not your friend's?" asked Naagin.

"Siya? My friend? HA! What a joke! I'm helping you, because Sir has promised me that I would receive a lot of fame and respect once he rises to power and gets the throne. And most importantly, I can get rid of my biggest enemy- Siya," said a very familiar voice. "She's always a champion in everything, always makes me feel inferior in front of her every success. Now, I will prove her that I'm better than her."

"Anika? No, it can't be her," whispered Siya to herself. "She will never think of me in this way. Never! That's just impossible!" But she could recognize the unmistakable voice to be her best friend's. Even though she was very afraid to face the people that she had just heard, she couldn't resist herself anymore to take a quick glance of the speakers. The bluestone had again started glowing for quite a long time, becoming brighter and brighter with every passing second. But Siya was too afraid of other things presently to notice the glow of her bluestone.

She slowly rose up from the rug on which she was lying, got the candle, walked past the closet, and peeped through the tiny crack. She caught sight of an attractive lady, whom she at once recognized as the woman on the Swan vehicle. She was in the same forest green mermaid gown, camouflaging herself with the deep green background (but her extra long dark green robe was thankfully absent this time). Next to her stood an exceptionally handsome man of about thirty, whose look was as charming and addictive as ever, but his eyes were full of cruelty and malice. And sure enough, beside these two adults was her best friend Anika, now saying, "All these years, I've been pretending to be her friend and well-wisher. But now I am tired. I can't maintain this fake friendship anymore."

This was enough to give Siya a trauma. She badly wanted someone to pinch her and tell that this was nothing, but just a nightmare. But she knew it wasn't, and the harsh reality now in front of her made her feel that she was going to break down completely.

"Danav, its time you have a word with our Siya," said Naagin. "Open!" she commanded, and the door started moving. Siya saw that her bluestone's glow was now at its peak. She grabbed it tightly and closed her eyes. "God, help me! Please save me!" she whispered, half wishing that the stone could work as her talisman.

Her ears told her that the door had sprung open, and her murderers were standing in the same room where she was. But her closed eyes showed her the silhouette of someone...of a boy, most probably.

And as she opened her eyes, the roof of the house vanished to show a dark sky, and a staircase emerged right where she was standing. "Siya, quick! Come up here," shouted out a boy.

"Abhilash! You here?" Siya asked, bewildered.

"No time for questions, hurry!" said Abhilash.

"Oh no! She is escaping!" cried out Naagin, as Siya dashed up the stairs and caught hold of the outspread hand of the real Mahashakti Rajeshwari, who instantly gave her a flying feather and motioned her to fly with her.

"ANIKA, WHAT ARE YOU DOING THERE? COME UP HERE, QUICK!" Udghoshak insisted, as Danav bellowed out with his deathwand, that had a spiteful skinny skeleton-hand with long nails protruding out of its upper tip, "Bars be around you!". And as he said so, the four of them; Siya, Abhilash, Udghoshak and Rajeshwari got locked inside a cage, as silver-grey bars formed around them to form an enclosure.

"Anika won't come," said Siya, as Udghoshak looked at her in a puzzled expression, clutching the silver-grey bars angrily. "She's changed sides."

"SO THAT'S WHY WE COULDN'T DETECT HER SAFETY," he said in annoyed realization.

In the meantime, Rajeshwari focused her hand to the centre point where the bars united, and yelled, "Melt the metal!" and the silver-grey bars liquefied and evaporated away.

"That was clever," uttered Danav in disgusted surprise, and rose his deathwand to cast another spell. But Naagin stopped him and advised, "Use quantity," which Siya couldn't decipher.

Rajeshwari pointed out into the dark below when they reached the edge of the roof, where Siya was almost about to trip at the sight that the roof on which she was standing belonged to a one-roomed house which was floating in the air, and there was no ground below the house. In fact, there were many more such houses which were bouncing in the dark. "Thanks God that it's not as black as it was down the cave, in our storeroom," thought Siya, as her white feather saved her from falling down. "Here we can at least see each other."

"Fly!" Rajeshwari cried out, and all four of them whooshed down the dark. "We have to reach The Great Black."

"That" Siya sighed with relief, "was a narrow escape!"

"Not escaped yet," said Rajeshwari. "Look behind!"

Abhilash and Siya turned around, and found out that they were being chased by swarms of creatures, who looked like zombies and ghosts and beasts that they had never imagined in their wildest dreams.

"GOOD HEAVENS!" puffed Udghoshak in horror. ***"DANAV HAS SET HALF HIS DEMONS BEHIND US!"***

"Oh, so this is what Naagin had meant by 'quantity'," thought Siya.

Some of them were mixtures of animals and humans, some of them animals and birds, some of them insects and humans, and some others were the blending of fishes and animals and birds. And some were of such complicated breeds that it was impossible to recognize which portion of their body belonged to which category. There were only three similarities among all of them that Siya could find out. One, that they were all hungrily chasing the foursome, especially Siya. Two, they all had wings which beat ferociously against the wind of the dark Andheri Jahan. And three, none of the creatures was anywhere near to pleasant or friendly, like a unicorn or mermaid or something like that. They were all dangerous and ghostly and rotten. Some of them did look like handsome humans, but their frowns made them no nearer to affable-looking.

"Fly faster!" Rajeshwari clamoured. "Siya, don't keep looking back, it's making you slow. Once we get across The Great Black, these demons won't be able to do anything."

The demons darted towards the four with their full might, as Rajeshwari kept closing her eyes every half minute and opening her eyelids to bolt fireballs at the demons from her hand, that made them disappear with strange screeches like 'hmarrahhhh' or 'vrooohhhhhh'

"We're almost there!" yelled Rajeshwari through the shoutings and shriekings of the angry uproaring demons behind them, as the horrible tornado-like figure whirled in huge circles, which Siya now recognized as The Great Black. "Be careful! Make sure to dive right through the centre."

First went in Udghoshak.

"Siya! Fly fast!" Rajeshwari shouted ahead of her, as Siya flew in a speed so high that she had not even travelled in an aeroplane.

She approached The Great Black, as she saw a werewolf catching Abhilash by his shirt sleeve. And in a flash, Rajeshwari chanted some spell at the werewolf that made him howl with pain, and he became extinct within a second. Abhilash swiftly flew into the centre point of The Great Black, followed by Siya and Rajeshwari. Siya had just entered the black tornado and almost thought happily with respite that she had now escaped from

Andheri Jahaan, that a long tail firmly caught hold of her leg, and prevented her from entering The Great Black. The creature gave a whack to Siya and tried to pull her back, in the process of which she dropped her feather.

Rajeshwari, who had gone into The Great Black, reappeared with fury and casted a fireball with such anger and force that five demons disappeared at once with shrieks of 'hmarrahhhh' and 'vrooohhhhhh'. Holding on to the feather in her left hand, and grasping Siya with her right (who was just about to fall), she flew at the speed of a race one car, and dived through The Great Black into the light of Jadooi Jahan, leaving the roaring demons in a frenzy of rage.

JADOOI JAHAN

"Are we now safe?" Siya asked.

"Yes," said Rajeshwari with a smile, as she called another flying feather to aid Siya in flying.

"THAT'S OUR ONLY ADVANTAGE AGAINST DANAV AND HIS LOT," said Udghoshak, ***"THAT THE DEMONS CAN'T STAND THE LIGHT OF OUR SHINES."***

"But I know that he will not sit idle," said Rajeshwari in a serious undertone. "He'll plan something or the other."

"You are the real Mahashakti Rajeshwari, aren't you?" asked Siya excitedly. Rajeshwari opened her mouth to say yes, but had to close it abruptly as Siya spoke again, "It's a great pleasure to meet you, Mahashakti Rajeshwari!"

Siya sprang her hands towards Rajeshwari, which she shook gently and opened her mouth to say that it was a pleasure for her too. But as soon as she had opened her mouth, she again had to close it as Siya interrupted her again, "Can I have a photo with you, Mahashakti?"

"Next she's going to ask you for autograph," chimed in Abhilash. "You've got a fan, MS!"

Rajeshwari opened her mouth to ask what's an autograph, but again had to press her lips, as Siya snapped, "You shut up, Abhilash! And how did you come here, by the way?"

"Never mind. It's a long story," said Abhilash.

"Followed you and Anika," said Rajeshwari, making Abhilash go red.

"Followed us? And who is MS?" Siya asked.

"Abbreviation for Mahashakti," replied Abhilash honestly.

"I know that!"

"Oh! I thought that you will think MS means Master of Science," said Abhilash in sarcasm. "Then why did you ask me?"

"Because she is the Great Queen of Jadooi Jahaan, she is the Mahashakti!"

"Oh really? I didn't know that," Abhilash said again in sarcasm. "Are you the queen of this place, MS?" he asked Rajeshwari. Rajeshwari in return only gave a smile. Udghoshak and she were undoubtedly enjoying the children's argument.

"She is not your friend that you will talk with her in that way!" Siya insisted. "You should address her with respect."

"She *is* my friend," protested Abhilash. "And she herself suggested me to call her so."

"Honestly Siya," said Rajeshwari, laughing, "I don't mind the least what someone calls me, unless and until I know that it's me who the person is referring to."

"Exactly," said Abhilash. "Even she is not bothered of what she is being called. Even you can call her with a nickname. Mahashakti Rajeshwari becomes too long."

"No, thankyou. I'm not a lazy lump of protoplasm like you!" said Siya with a scowl and turned her face away from Abhilash.

"You are not welcome!" replied Abhilash with a same scowl, and turned his face away.

"WHY ARE YOU SHAKING YOUR HAND?" asked Udghoshak. **"IS THERE SOME PROBLEM WITH IT?"**

"It looks like a snake bite, isn't it?" asked Siya, showing Udgjoshak and Rajeshwari her left hand with two spots of black on it. "Maybe Naagin cast a snake spell on me. The pain had died, but now it's again hurting."

"Oh Goodness! She actually bit you!" exclaimed Rajeshwari in a pained way. "How dare she!" Rajeshwari cursed in rage.

"She bit me?" asked Siya bewildered, as Rajeshwari closed her eyes and muttered something with her hands fisted near her mouth. "Is she a vampire or something?"

"NAAGIN IS A REPTILADY," explained Udghoshak, as Siya saw Rajeshwari blowing some kind of magic dust on her left hand, which instantly made the black spots vanish and her hand didn't hurt anymore. **"PART REPTILE, PART WOMAN. A VERY FEW OF THE SPECIES EXIST TODAY".**

"Thank you!" said Siya gratefully.

"You are always welcome," returned Rajeshwari in a pleasured smile.

Siya then looked down, and as soon as she did, her face at once lit up and she exclaimed, "Oh, look! This is so beautiful!"

"Wow!," Abhilash looked at the breathtaking view of Jadooi Jahan in wonder. "Simply WOW!"

"Let's fly down, please!," Siya requested.

"Where do you think that we are going?," asked Rajeshwari, as Siya now realized that had been swooping downwards all the time.

"Udghoshak will do the honours to be your guide," said Rajeshwari, as Siya and Abhilash looked down at the amazing place in complete fascination. And Udghoshak happily chattered about almost everything that Siya and Abhilash saw, all the way to Shakti Bhawan.

"THIS HUGE TREE YOU SEE HERE," said Udghoshak proudly, ***"IS ARPITA, ALSO KNOWN AS THE GREAT GIVER."***

"Yes! I had read about it in the ittila," Siya said excitedly.

"I doubt if there's anything left in the world that you haven't read," jeered Abhilash.

"And that over there is the crying hut, right?" Siya continued, ignoring Abhilash's comments.

"THAT'S RIGHT," said Udghoshak.

"I read that too in the Ittila!"

"And the noble prize in the category of 'Hut Identification' goes to Siya Sharma!" Abhilash derisioned again and clapped his hands in mockery, as if he was actually announcing the name of a noble prize winner and summoning the winner to come up onto the stage.

Rajeshwari opened her mouth to ask what a noble prize meant, but Siya, her eternal interrupter again forced her to seal her lips and snapped, "And the gold medal in Olympics for making the highest score in unnecessary mockery goes to non other than- the one and only- Abhilash Malhotra!"

Abhilash sulked and looked at the view below. The flowers were as tall as a building, their leaves the size of Rafflesia. The streets were full of lisams, who by their looks were not any different from humans, winged and non winged pixies, and lovely wonderful creatures that were of such a huge variety that it was difficult to describe all of them.

"What are those, Udghoshak?" asked Abhilash, relieved that Siya didn't know about it and looked down with the same curiosity as him, and pointed towards a group of spheres, small and large, dull and bright, old and new, some on ground and some swaying in air.

"THIS IS WHERE THE SETTLEMENT STARTS," stated Udghoshak. *"AND THESE ARE THE DWELLINGS, WHERE THE LISAMS AND PIXIES LIVE."*

"They are so pretty!" ejaculated Siya.

"SO THEY ARE," agreed Udghoshak. *"AND THAT GREAT SPONGY THING, WHERE YOU CAN SEE SO MANY PEOPLE SPRAWLING AND LOUNGING... IT'S CALLED THE LAZYLISAM'S BAG. THAT'S THE PLACE WHERE YOU CAN JUST LOLL AND DROWSE CONTENDEDLY ALL DAY LONG, AND EVEN THE QUEEN CAN'T DISTURB SOMEONE WHILE RESTING THERE."*

"Sharda's dream destination!" joked abhilash. And all of them burst out laughing, including Siya, even if two out of the four didn't know who Sharda was.

Till the Shakti Bhawan, they examined everything that attracted their eye below them, with Siya and Abhilash asking what's this and what's that, and Udghoshak pleasantly educating them, *"THAT LITTLE THING YOU SEE OVER THERE...YOU SEE THAT, THAT'S A...DO YOU KNOW WHAT THAT'S CALLED...THIS ORANGE THING YOU SEE...,"* and Abhilash cracking a joke every now and then that made everyone stop on their way to laugh, and Siya exclaiming in half of the things, "Yes! Yes! I also read about that in the Ittila!."

It was only after the huge magnificent castle came into view that Siya and Abhilash fell silent in adoration of the splendid white-blue piece of architecture, and Usghoshak proclaimed, *"WHAT YOU ARE SEEING RIGHT NOW IS THE SHAKTI BHAWAN, THE ROYAL PALACE OF JADOOI JAHAN. AND THAT SPARKLING TOPMOST POINT, WHICH IS SHAPED LIKE A STAR, AND PLACED RIGHT IN FRONT OF THE CASTLE IS –*

"The Amarshikha"

"YOU'RE RIGHT," said Udghoshak.

"If she's ever wrong, I'll change my name!" said Abhilash.

As they neared the Shakti Bhawan, they found out that a huge crowd was standing on their way to the castle, some of them on the ground and some in the air, all looking suspectively at the two strangers, wanting to stop them and interrogate them, but made way for them when they saw Mahashakti Rajeshwari herself leading them to the Shakti Bhawan.

Shakti Bhawan was what could be thought of as the tenth power of the Taj Mahal. They saw a gate that was half the height of Qutub Minar, and paused in front of it.

"Touch this," said Rajeshwari, showing Siya and Abhilash a glowing purple-pink flower each. They obediently touched the flowers, and the flowers disappeared. "This is a sign that you have not broke out into the palace, and that you have decent permission to enter the castle grounds," she elaborated. They then entered the enormous gateway, which disappeared when they walked into it, and reappeared once they were inside the campus of Shakti Bhawan. Surrounded by glass fountains that swished waves of what looked like fire, vast gardens with sky-touching flowers and lovely creatures, Shakti Bhawan in a total was a second name for beauty. And as Udghoshak had very correctly spelled out, right in front of the castle was a tower taller than Dubai's Burj Khalifa, with a peak shaped like a five pointed star whose brightness by all means had no match.

They walked into the palace to discover that its interior was just as beautiful as it's exterior. The glass roofs were supported with star shaped crystal pillars, and the flight of stairs lead them into rooms so large that it could have fit Siya's entire house.

"You can choose any of these rooms, except the last one of course, as it is the armour room. You can have rest if you want."

"We don't want rest," Siya said immediately, and then added, "at least, I don't."

"Same here," said Abhilash.

"Mahashakti," said Siya politely, "if you are not tired, and if you don't mind, can you please spare some minutes with me? Because I think I really need to talk to you about a number of things."

"I am of course not tired at all. And when you think that you need to talk to me, there's no chance that I'm going to say no. So tell me, is there anything that is troubling you?"

"Yes, I –

"NOW SIYA, ABHILASH, I MUST INSIST THAT FIRST YOU TWO AT LEAST CHOOSE A ROOM FOR YOURSELVES, SO THAT I CAN APPOINT A PAIR OF GUARD PIXIES THERE."

"I'll take this one," said Siya, pointing to the room in front of which they were standing, without thinking or inspecting the room. "It looks alright to me."

"I'll take the next one, then," said Abhilash, not even throwing a glance at it.

"YOU TWO WILL ALSO HAVE TO GO THROUGH A NUMBER OF TESTS, TO PROVE TO THE PEOPLE THAT YOU ARE WELL-WISHERS OF JADOOI JAHAN."

"Chuck the tests, Udghoshak," said Rajeshwari. "I think it will be better not to mention to the people that they are humans. If someone asks, then we'll just tell them that these kids are orphans, and that I like them, so I kept them here."

"FINE. AS YOU WISH. I'M OFF TO GET HOLD OF TWO PIXIES, WHO WILL GUARD YOU AND HELP YOU IN ANYTHING YOU NEED. SEE YOU SOON."

"Bye," said Siya automatically, and then instantly turned to Rajeshwari to talk.

"So I –

"Wait Siya, let's go to my room upstairs," said Rajeshwari. "And there we can sit and talk. Yeah?"

"Yeah," replied Siya, and they climbed up the stairs to Rajeshwari's room, which was, by no doubt, another piece of divine architecture, guarded by two chattering grey-frocked pixies who stood to attention when Rajeshwari entered, eyed Siya and Abhilash with narrowed eyelids, and again began chattering once they were all in.

"Sit here, kids," she beckoned them to a maroon sofa. "Now tell me. What has been bothering you?"

"My best friend, Mahashakti," said Siya. "I'm sure they have done something to her. She behaved very oddly today morning in that place…what did you call it…yes, Andheri Jahan. She told that she had been faking the friendship with me all these years. She was not the Anika I know of, Mahashakti. They've certainly done something to her."

"I know it's not easy to accept betrayal from someone to whom you are so close, but Siya –

"SHE – DID – NOT –BETRAY – ME!" Siya yelled, which made Rajeshwari quite taken aback. "I am sorry. Extremely sorry. I know I shouldn't have talked like that. But I know my friend. She just can't be like what I saw," said Siya, almost on the verge of tears. No matter how much her heart didn't want to accept the reality, her mind knew very well that Anika most obviously wasn't a real friend, and indeed a very excellent actress who had faked the friendship only to earn a buddy she could pass her time with, and to get all the name and fame as being the friend of a girl really famous in the school. It was hard to see the truth.

"How could she change so much?" asked Siya, as if asking the question to herself.

Rajeshwari advised, "You must have heard of the quote, *'It's not the people who change, it's only their mask that falls off'*."

How could I never know, thought Siya.

To provide condolence, Rajeshwari said, "Um…maybe she'll recover from whatever spell they have cast on her? Maybe we can treat her with the Amruta of the healing pond. Its water cures terrible to terrible disorders."

"Maybe," said Siya, holding back a sob, and then started crying hysterically. Abhilash looked awkwardly sideways as Rajeshwari came near Siya and patted her head, trying all her best to comfort her.

"Don't cry, dear," consoled Rajeshwari. "No, don't cry."

"You know what Anika will say if she sees you crying like this?" asked Abhilash. "She'll say that you would make a great role for one of those always-crying daughter in laws of a serial."

"Well, that's true," thought Siya, and smiled.

"Mahashakti, why don't you tell us something about Danav?," said Siya inquisitively, as the idea suddenly struck her mind. "I mean, how did he become so powerful? And when you have got such a huge army, then why don't you just squash him up? The Ittila tells that there are about some twenty thousand rakshaks devoted for Jadooi Jahan's defence forces, which includes excellent lisams, first rate pixies, and all kinds of creatures starting from a tiny bunnymouse to a gigantic mammothosoraus, who are just as brilliant as the lisams. When he is such a threat to Jadooi Jahan that innocent lives have to face mortal perils, then why don't you fight against him and his demons and finish him off?"

I WANT PROOF

"You think it's a child's game to finish off Rajeshwari, don't you Naagin dear?" said Danav, sitting on a large red velvet couch, his feet resting on a glowing red mammothosoraus skin, as Anika surveyed the spherical dome-like room with an even redder wallpaper, which showed a humangous long nailed witched hand, the sign of Andheri Jahan.

"Do you realize that our demons are highly sensitive to light?" asked Danav. "And that Jadooi Jahan is full of shines that KILL the darkness, and so also the dark POWER within them?"

"I do, but –

"What but, huh? Where does a but come here at all?" barked Danav furiously. "In order to get Jadooi Jahan's throne, Naagin, we will have to desroy the Shakti stupa's star, for which the white fire burning in it has to be extinguished. But I unfortunately didn't know this at the time when I was eighteen. I thought that only the truthwand would do the job. And the Shakti stupa is the brightest shine of the entire magical world. When you get close to such a bright object, even a lisam becomes unconscious, and burnt if one goes too close to it. And we are just demons, and you a reptilady. How shall we ever get there?"

"Should I ask the searcher if it knows something about it?"

"Yes, please do. But I don't think you will get any information that can come in our use."

"What is a searcher?" asked Anika curiously, "if I may ask?," she adjoined the second bit on looking at Danav who gave her a nasty look and then answered, "Just the way you have google search engine, searcher is a talking skull which gives information about many things, but certainly not all. Well that is a different thing, but I don't see why I should keep you alive. You have not been of any use to us till now, except for speaking bad about your ex-best friend Siya. Do you deny that?," he asked coldly.

"I don't deny that, my Lord!" said Anika with overwhelming emotions. "But you won't get the information about Siya on the searcher, which I can give you."

"I don't need any information about Siya," Danav was barking again. "I will simply kill her with the Kaala Jal. Her existence reminds me of my failure. And now that she has so willingly walked into the jaws of death, how can I deny her help when she is seeking me the path to heaven?" said Danav triumphantly. "She has done a big mistake by coming here. She does not know that by entering the magical world, she herself has written death in her destiny," he articulated. "If you want to help, then just tell me one thing. Are you really against Siya, and the lisams?"

"Of course, yes, my Lord!" said Anika at once.

"Then prove it!" snarled Danav.

"How do I prove it, my Lord?" asked a frightened Anika in a small voice. "I have already expressed my hatred towards Siya. Believe me! I can do anything to defeat her."

"Just saying that won't do. You will have to appear through a small test."

"Wh...wh...what test, my Lord?" asked Anika in a very terrified voice.

"You see that black skeleton-hand on the wall?" asked Danav in a very cunning voice.

"Yes, Lord. I do," she replied obediently.

"Go there and lean against it," said Danav, as he happily saw every muscle on Anika's body flinch. "Come on, go there. Nothing will happen to you."

Anika slowly walked to the wall, and leaned against it.

"See? Nothing happened," said Danav, and then curved his lips to an evil smile, "But things can happen if you do something that does not please me. You understand?"

"Yes," said Anika.

"Good. So you love telling how much you hate Siya, don't you? Now stand there and tell me five things which you hate the most about Siya. And remember: one lie, and the death hand will slice your throat with its nails. It doesn't take more than a knife to take a human's life, does it?," he said, his smile broadened. "Now. START!"

Anika took a very deep breath, and said, "I hate it when my mom compares me to Siya and scolds me about how perfect Siya is, and how imperfect I am. I hate it when everyone claps after listening to Siya's song, but no one even throws a glance at my sketches. I hate her when she promises to come to my house to help me with my homework, but doesn't come. She says that she had to stay home for some or the other important work. I hate her when she lies to me. I… I hate it when…when…

"Speak fast, I haven't got all day for you," blustured Danav.

"I…I hate it when she ignores me, and pays more attention to someone whom I don't like."

"No doubt that every word you spoke was true," said Danav. "But I don't think there was a lot of hatred in your voice."

"I was so scared that I couldn't think what to tell. Lord, I don't know if you trust me or not, but I must say that I want Siya to be dead and defeated as soon as possible. So I think I will start telling you things that you might want to know. She has got a bluestone, which must be a very powerful element –

"What did you say? She has got the bluestone?" asked Danav. "This knowledge can surely help us know a thing or two about Jadooin Jahan's messiah. Thankyou, Anika. If you said that about Siya, I am sure that you hate her from the very core of your heart."

"My Lord, why don't you tell me about your victorious past?" requested Anika.

"Why so?" asked Danav in a thunderous tone.

"Becaue…because..I want to learn from you. I want to take your inspiration. I have heard a lot about your glory, Lord. I want to know how the Great Demon God rose to power. I just…I just want to know about you and your brave achievements, my Lord."

"Even I would like to know about it, Danav," said Naagin, making a sudden entry with her skullwand. "You have never told me clearly of what had happened on the ninety ninth day of 15th October, 1999."

15th OCTOBER, 1999

After a lot of thinking and overthinking, Rajeshwari spoke, "Once upon a time there used to be a day, when I and my sister Maahi played together, danced together, learnt spells together, and lived together. I did not know what in the world was called sorrow. My world only consisted of brightness and colours.

"Mahashakti Maheshwari, that is, my elder sister Maahi, was the queen of Jadooi Jahan. The day I am talking about, dated the ninety ninth of 15th October, 1999, was when my life had to start a new journey. It was the day which changed my life forever."

As Siya was new to the character of Maheshwari, she began listening to Rajeshwari more intently.

"The day I'm talking about was the day of the auspicious occasion of Rang Festival, the festival of colours."

"Are you talking about Holi?" asked Siya. "In India, we also celebrate the festival of colours, we call it Holi."

"Oh, do you? Well, then you can possibly imagine what a happy occasion it is," said Rajeshwari.

"There were colours everywhere, choking the atmosphere," said Danav. "Clouds were swinging and dancing madly, and supplying irksome colourful dust sprays and water colours everywhere. People were so engrossed in enjoying themselves that no one noticed me. Everything was just as I had expected, and things till now for me had gone according to plan. So I just waited in queue for my turn to give my present to the queen."

"Everything was going perfectly," said Rajeshwari. "But who knew that this Rang Festival was going to be played with blue only. What I mean here by blue is blood, because blue blood was what the castle was drenched in on that day."

"Blue blood?" asked Siya in surprise.

"Your blood's colour is red, isn't it? In the same way, every Lisam's and pixie's blood, and every animal and bird's blood here is blue in colour. This day was the beginning of darkness in the magical world. Crime took a new face, that Jadooi Jahan was not familiar with since thousands of years. Cruelty took an entirely new dimension, and pixie-murder became a part of daily news. It was soon when terror of Danav spread to every zone, his fear settled in every heart, and his name associated with a shudder before being pronounced by every tongue."

Seeing Abhilash put a hand on his mouth to stop yawning, and Siya giving her a you-are –so-insensitive-to-people's-feelings look, she said, "I'm sorry. I know I ran a bit off-track. So as I was saying, all the Lisams and pixies were in a very happy mood. Everyone was enjoying.

"Large bubbles of dust colours and water colours were being sprinkled from the merrily back-and-forth rocking clouds. For me, the enjoyment was double. When I wished, I flew down to Jadooi Jahan's common grounds, and danced and played with other common people. And when I wished, I ran back to the Shakti Bhawan, and sat down in the Assembly Hall with Maahi and other Royal members to enjoy the shows put up by people from near and far, and gifts that were mostly presented to the kingdom by people who came from distant and far off lands. And as a h   h being the Mahashakti presented the artists e   s with gold and diamonds.

w that one of these artists in the queue had ncrease the brilliance of the occasion, but to opposite of it! After a group of six amazing came Danav in the disguise of an extremely old man, claiming his identity as Shivsen from a far off Anokhi Jahan. What he had come to do, was something we were all curious to see. Because he told that he was a future teller.

"The first thing that he said on coming to the dais was, 'This lovely girl sitting next to you, Mahashakti, is just as pretty as you. Is she your sister?'

"'Yes, Sir Shivsen. She is my younger sister,' Maahi replied with a smile.

"'Ah, your sister. Looks very similar to you,' Danav said, or should I say, Shivsen.

"'Wait, I can't allow you to touch the truthwand,' said Maahi, because Shivsen was actually progressing towards the wand of the throne, the truthwand.

"And Danav's reason was this, 'But for telling the future, I need to hold the truthwand, and I need to focus all my concentration on it. It will show me the clearest vision of Jadooi Jahan's future.' Maahi suggested him to stand in the centre of the Shakti on the Assembly Hall's floor. Because Shakti, Jadooi Jahan's sign, with the picture of Amarshikha in it, is not just a mere sign; it has immense powers.

"But Danav's aim was the truthwand, and so he went on buttering, 'On such a happy occasionlike the Rang Festival, please don't stop me from presenting you with this small gift. I have been working on this for my whole life, Mahashakti. Just give me one chance to take you into th journey of future, and I assure you that you will be delighte with my work. Please, your highness, just one chance!'

"He was pleading so profusely, that anyone woul have bestowed kindness upon him. Even I was so excite about seeing a future telecast, that I had also began begging Maahi to grant him the permission. Finally Maahi agreed, 'Then I would not stop you, Sir. No one in my kingdom has seen a future telecast before. I will not make you upset. You have my permission. You can have the truthwand.'

"*You can have the truthwand.* I still regret asking Maahi to allow Danav to hold the wand, because otherwise she probably wouldn't have told these words. As everyone in the Assembly Hall eagerly watched the old future teller walking towards the truthwand and picking it up, the aged Shivsen pulled out his beard, took out his false moustache and removed the stupid traveller cloth which he had wrapped around his head the moment he set his hands on the truthwand. Now in front of us was a young handsome man of eighteen. And then with a thunderous laugh that had shaken the hall, and echoes in my nightmares till today, he pulled me as offensively as he could have and put the wand at my throat. The courtiers had now angrily pulled out their weapons, but they all backed off when Danav gave another blood-wrenching laugh and spat, 'Now, the truthwand is mine. And now, I am the king of Jadooi Jahan. I have complete faith that none of you will move from your place. Because if you do, I will slaughter this young lady.'

"Danav had thought that seizing the truthwand would make him the emperor of Jadooi Jahan. But establishing his rule in Jadooi Jahan needed the Amarshikha to be unlighted. And it was evident that he didn't know it. So thinking that he had already gained the victory, he raised the wand up in the air in triumph and announced, 'I have won the truthwand, my demons. Now make all these big-headed Lisams and filthy pixies of Jadooi Jahan praise my name. And if they don't, then let them know my power, and just kill them. The king of a land is known to be the God of the land. Let blue rivers of blood flow across Jadooi Jahan, if the citizens of Jadooi Jahan don't wish to worship their God.' And the demons exactly did what their master had ordered- they killed. The shrieks of pain and the cries of agony that I had heard that day still disturb me whenever I think of Danav.

"I sometimes think how I have remembered all these dialogues so accurately. But the truth is…I never have to recall these dialogues while narrating this story. Because the incidents of that day had got so deeply embedded in my heart, that the brain never had to memorize it.

"But my favourite of all these dialogues was what my sister had said to Danav, 'If you want the throne of Jadooi Jahan, then why did you come here in disguise? If you have courage, then fight with me like a true warrior.'"

"'A true warrior is one who has brains, and knows how to win the battle,' I said. Now it seemed that Jadooi Jahan, the biggest empire of the magical world, was under my rule. But Maheshwari, as well as her little sister Rajeshwari were more clever and stubborn than I had expected.

"I told Rajeshwari that I would pardon her life, if she just uttered one thing: 'I accept defeat from you'. But this little idiot only infuriated my nerves. Even though she was just a twelve year old kid, she still cared more for her prestige than her life; she told me that she would rather have her head slashed, but she won't bow her head. She said she would fight to her death, but would not bend in front of me.

"In the meantime when I had not noticed, Maheshwari had already chanted the summoning spell on the Kaala Jal, the black water, which could only have been summoned by an extremely talented lisam."

"'It's a sincere request to everyone present here, please disperse,' said Maahi. 'I will deal with this myself. You all go and help the army fight the demons.'

"Everyone started moving, but stiffened when they heard Danav say, 'No one moves a step, or else I will kill your Mahashakti's sister.'

"Just one glance at Maahi's eyes, and I understood what she was trying to do. She had summoned the Kaala Jal, and now she wanted to transfer it to me. I knew which charm had to be used: the blink-and-send charm. I stared into her eyes carefully, at the same time trying all my best not to attract Danav's eyes, as she mouthed one…two..

"And at the count of three, we blinked together, and the next moment the glass bottle containing the Kaala Jal was in my hand. 'It's your Mahashakti's order,' Maahi shouted in a blasted sort of voice, and all the courtiers very hesitantly moved out of the Assembly Hall. I quickly raised the Kaala Jal in front of Danav so that he could see it clearly, and whispered in his ear, 'You will not kill me, or my sister. Because if you do, the Pavitra Pushpa's job is to bring back dead royal families back to their life. But do you know what will happen to you if I pour this Kaala Jal on you? Even a single drop of this poison will take your life for once and forever, and world's no healing flower or Amruta will be able to save you after that.'"

"Then I applied my brains. I kneeled down before her and grabbed her feet, and started begging for mercy. I started pretending that I had accepted defeat, had realized my mistakes, and that I wanted a second chance. My plan was to make her believe that I had really seen through my wrong deeds and that I had totally surrendered, so that I could grab any opportunity to snatch the Kaala Jal from her, and wipe out the sisters forever.

"But it seemed that fooling them once again was not possible. When I realized that I had no choices left and that Rajeshwari had already opened the lid of the bottle to kill me, I did what I could have done only once in my life. I used my last-choice-charm. And using this charm, I cast the supertrap spell on Maheshwari, because that was the only thing that I could then think of to ensure my survival."

"Danav bellowed joyfully, with his evil smirk on his attractive face, 'Now your sister will be trapped inside me, forever. And I am sure that you won't do any harm to her, and thus I too will remain unharmed.'

"I stood spellbound as I tried to take in what had just happened in front of me. Because the spell that he had cast on Maahi was something that we knew only to exist in tales and legends. Then Danav again burst out, 'Now you would not be able to talk to your sister at all, not even through mind-to-mind connect charm, because now she will be a part of me.'

"Realizing that I was going to lose my sister forever, I stood there shaking from head to toe, and the Kaala Jal fell off from my hand, which Danav caught before it could have crashed on the floor. Danav was again speaking with his evil grin, 'You have the last two minutes of your life to spend with her. Tell her goodbye.'

"I looked agonizingly at Maahi, whose feet had already started disappearing. Then Maahi also used the last-choice-charm, and created you Siya. And when the reason of the creation was asked, she said 'Messiah of Jadooi Jahan, destruction of Danav and end of crime'. I was again feeling hopeful. This creation was just a superb idea. Danav became mad at this, as he knew that the creation of a soul always resulted in the reason of its creation turning into reality.

"'It was you who had come as the future teller, but now it's me who has written your future with my creation,' Maahi said. But he did not want to die. And as soon as the newly created soul started its travel into some body, Danav cast a spell on your soul that made you powerless. And this was the end of all my hopes. Because this meant that you were going to be born somewhere which would have very less magical properties. But I had not expected you to be totally non-magical. No doubt that Danav's spell had been very very strong.

"Now Maahi was visible only upto her chest. Before leaving me, she said, 'In the human world, they say that after every dark night, there's a sunrise, whose light clears the dark. Don't lose hope. Five years, Eight years, Ten years, Fifteen years, however much time it takes…just wait!' After saying this, her face also disappeared slowly. Danav was desperately wanting to kill me, now that he also had the Kaala Jal. But maybe it was your presence, Siya, maybe it was your soul's brightness of holiness and sanity that stopped Danav from daring to do me any harm. I don't what happened to you after that. What I believe according to logical possibilities is that your soul travelled to the solar system straight away, and entered the planet Earth through your house's storeroom, because that storeroom is the connection between your planet and the magical land. At least that's what I think. It must have made a lot of storm and flooding in that room, due to the sudden loss of magical powers, and then it would have entered your mother's womb. Problably that's the reason why your mom thinks that the storeroom is dangerous, as that day she must have heard and saw a lot of unusual things there. So, for your safety, she locked the storeroom and didn't allow anyone to enter there henceforth. But I see that the lock didn't stop your soul's urge to complete the mission that it was created for. Well anyways, that's the story, and then Danav flew off with the truthwand and the Kaala Jal, leaving me in doom and depression.

"And then one day, Naagin love, you came into my life like a new weapon of power. That was when you had prayed me that you wanted me to accept you as my life companion, and I had told you to prove yourself worthy of me. And it was impressive that a reptilady, a species which was believed to be weak and useless and almost on the verge of extinction had that day become successful in stealing the Pavitra Pushpa for me. I couldn't stop myself from falling for you, Naagin. Because from then, you were not only my support, you had become my necessity.

"Talking about Maheshwari, she in my opinion had decided to become a dumb in her next birth, and was probably doing a regular practise for the same. Because my royal captive never ever opened her mouth to talk to me, not even when I spent hours trying to make her talk. But one fine day, suddenly an idea surged into her mind, and she asked me, 'What if I kill myself? You will die, won't you?'

"Well, the answer was obvious." I said cooly, 'You will not kill yourself, because if you do so then my Naagin will convert herself into you and go kill your sister.' You know Anika, these sisters loved each other so much, that they were ready to sacrifice their lives for one another. But that was a good thing for me anyways, because this only sentence was enough to make her silent.

"I couldn't tell anyone about Maahi's capture because, they would not have believed it, except Udghoshak of course. Whatever be my problem, Udghoshak was always there to stand by me. This type of spell had earlier happened only in legends and tales, but never in reality. If I would have said this to anyone, they would have thought that I was going crazy from depression or something."

"A LISAM WHO HAD SUSPICIOUSLY OVERHEARD OUR CONVERSATION WANTED TO DIRECTLY GO AND KILL DANAV," joined Udghoshak at the end of the story telling. The three had become so engrossed in the story, that they hadn't even realized when Udghoshak had come back. *"IT TOOK A LOT OF EFFORT TO PUT THE ANTI-MEMORY CHARM ON HIM, SO THAT HE WOULD FORGET ABOUT THE INCIDENT."*

"So, we could never attack Danav, never take our revenge. And the whole Jadooi Jahan was really furious about this."

"NOW, I THINK IT'S TIME TO GO TO BED. THE PIXIES WILL BE ARRIVING SHORTLY.MAYBE YOU'LL GET TO SEE THEM TOMORROW. NOW OFF YOU GO, YOU TWO."

LIBRARY - SOLUTION TO ALL PROBLEMS

"Good afternoon, time to wake up!" said a little pink furred pixie.

"Jenny, it should be good evening! In their world there's a sun which sets during the evening."

"No Jack," said a blue furred pixie. "I guess it should be goodnight. Because they have a night in earth after the day."

"Jenny, you are so confusing! Just now you said that it's afternoon, and now you are saying that it's night."

"Goodmorning!" said Siya, yawning with half closed eyes.

"Good morning!" squealed out the two little pixies, both at the same time.

"Hello! I am Jack, and she is my brother Jenny," said Jack.

"No, I am jenny, her sister, I mean- his sister," said Jenny.

"Actually, I am his brother, sorry her brother," said Jack. "And he, I mean she- is my sister."

"Look, look, look. Actually, he is Jack, my sister. No, no, not sister, my brother. And –

"Wait. Let me tell," said Siya, who was confusedly looking from Jack to Jenny and Jenny to Jack. "So you are Jack," Siya guessed correctly, cupping the football sized sky-blue furred pixie, who delightfully hopped in Siya's arms excitedly.

"And you are Jenny," she said.

"Yes!," joyfully cried Jenny, the pink furred pixie and did a small pirouette around Siya, leaving a trail of sparkling fluorescent pixie dust. Siya longingly looked at the rapidly disappearing dust.

"So you are the brother, and you are the sister. Am I correct?"

Jack and Jenny looked at each other with amazed expressions, as if Siya had crcked out the world's biggest mystery, and bluffed out, "YOU ARE CORRECT!," both at the exact same time.

"You two are so cute!" said Siya.

"THANK YOU!," squealed out the pixies, again at the same time, this time even more loudly and excitedly.

"'Morning!" said Abhilash, coming inside Siya's room.

"It's bad habit to come inside someone else's room without knocking," stated Siya, in what she and Anika called a superior-sort-of-joke voice.

"Oh really?" said Abhilash, walking back to the door. Knocking on it with an exceptional loud bang, he spoke, "May I come in, Madam?"

"Come in," said Siya in the same superior voice. "Making loud noises is also bad manners."

"According to you, is there any good manner in me at all?" he asked as he sat down on the pink couch near the bed, with Jack and Jenny on either side of him.

"Yes. You are very funny. And you are so cool."

"Really?" asked Abhilash very flattered, going a bit pink.

"You are brave," continued Siya. "Yesterday you rescued me from Andheri Jahan. Of course, Mahashakti also saved me. And I like your sense of humour, though you mostly use it to insult me."

"Not to insult you. But you are just so much of a miss perfect, you know."

"No one on earth is perfect," said Siya. "If I were perfect, I would have won the trophy in all the competitions. If I were perfect, my mom would have scolded me less for my disobedience and carelessness. If I were perfect, Anika would have never let me down in our friendship. If I were perfect, probably I should have already saved Jadooi Jahan from Danav's threats."

"My heart says that we can save Jadooi Jahan. And we will do it," said Abhilash determined. Siya nodded with a smile.

"We will do it!" repeated Jack and Jenny in a chorus.

"But what can we do?" asked Siya, thinking hard.

"Hey Jack and Jenny, do you have any ideas?" asked Abhilash. The pixies nodded their heads in disapproval.

"You know, Siya?" said he. "Jack was actually appointed as my guard. But he wanted to be your guard, the messiah's guard. And Jenny was surely not going to give her prestigious duty to Jack." The two pixies went red, and were giving toothy grins.

"Then they suddenly got into a cat fight. Messiah... messiah...messiah, that was the only word that I could catch from their argument. I don't know how you fell asleep so easily. Maybe you were very tired. But these two siblings went blah blah blah, and I sat there on my bed awake, waiting for them to shut up. And they didn't. So I told both of them to go and guard you. And it seems they are very happy to be your security."

"But why do we need a security?" asked Siya.

"To protect you from being carried away by a demon, of course," said Abhilash.

"Ohh"

A thought suddenly struck her mind. "Is there a library or something here?" asked Siya to the pixies.

"Library, seriously Siya?" asked Abhilash.

"Library?" asked Jack.

"What's a library?" asked Jenny.

"Oh, sorry. You call it Granthalaya. Is there a granthalaya here?"

"Many," said the pixies in chorus again, vigorously nodding their heads in a yes.

"Siya, books are not the solution to all problems."

"Can I go there?" asked Siya, ignoring Abhilash.

"I think so," said Jenny.

"Have to ask Mahashakti," said Jack.

"Can you please go and see if she is not busy?" asked Siya to the pixies. "And if I can talk to her about this?"

"Your job will be done," said Jack in a very serious tone, which appeared rather funny. "You stay guard, partner," he said to Jenny.

"Right, partner," said Jenny, also in a very serious tone, and Jack went fluttering at top speed to the open door and hit someone, as a result of which he fell on the floor with a gentle thud. He irritably rubbed his head and looked up angrily to see who had come in his way.

"Oh, I am sorry," said Rajeshwari. Looking at the Mahashakti, he at once stood to attention.

"Mahashakti, I was just thinking about you now," said Siya.

"Really?" asked Rajeshwari. "That's great, then."

"Mahashakti, I was thinking if I could have gone to a granthalya. I really know a very little about Jadooi Jahan. If I go through some books, maybe we can come across something that might help us in fighting Danav?"

"Why, that's a brilliant idea! I don't know how far that will help. But if you are eager to find out something from the library, then that's really worth a try. Because very few people in Jadooi Jahan are interested in books."

"Very few people in the world, not only Jadooi Jahan," said Abhilash.

"But that's a good idea, Siya. Check the Royal Granthalaya, it's in the third floor. Jack and Jenny will take you there. You can go there using the will charm, no need to climb all the way up the stairs."

"But I don't know how to work a charm."

"Oh, it's simple. Since you are not a lisam, put your hand around your amulet, and close your eyes, and tell your amulet what you want to do."

"That's it?" asked Abhilash and Siya together. They looked at each other, and then laughed.

"I think it's the influence of Jack and Jenny," said Abhilash.

"Yeah!" agreed Siya.

"Yes, that's it," assured Rajeshwari. "Then you don't have to climb up there."

Siya and Abhilash exactly did the same, and in no time found themselves moving up and crossing the glass roofs as if they were ghosts. Jack and Jenny willingly led them to the Royal Granthalaya, and Siya at once started pouring through books one after another. Abhilash, who was not much into books, chatted with the pixies. After sometime he decided to help Siya, and went to read from the section that she was readibg, labelled as *'ways to end evil powers'*. But it was not more than five minutes that he began to feel drowsy.

"It's so boring, Siya. How did you manage to read all that?" he asked, pointing at the pile of Siya's already-read extremely thick books.

"Just the way I read history civics," replied Siya. "It's boring, but still you have to read it."

"Hey Siya! Look at this," Abhilash called excitedly, pulling out a book named, *'Geography of Jadooi Jahan'*.

"What?" Siya came running to look at the book, thinking that Abhilash had really found something interesting.

"Look at this picture of the Healing Pond. It has been written below it that it is one thousand, four hundred and thirty six meter long. Let's invite Danav to a swimming party in it, and then we'll push him into the water, so that he drowns and dies there." Siya rolled her eyes most fractiously, and went back to lose herself in the books.

"Well, look at this. This book says about different designs of robes available currently in the magical world. Maybe we can replace one of his garments with an undersize robe. Then he will look all fat and bulky in it, and his girlfriend Naagin will then desert him. Then Danav will probably go into depression. And after that, he will commit suicide."

Siya gave no response.

"Okay, this one is really helpful. This tells about delicious mouth-watering cookies. Add poison to it, and serve it to Danav. He will be dead."

"You have come here to help me, or to disturb me?" snapped Siya.

"I'm trying to help you. See here, this book is about how to fly," said Abhilash. "Maybe we can find a spell on how to make a flying person fall, and then apply that on Danav. He'll fall and break all his 206 bones and die. Ha ha, so simple."

"Have you had your breakfast today, Abhilash?" asked Siya.

"That's a weird question. Of course I haven't because one doesn't feel hungry in Jadooi Jahan."

"So that's why you are eating my head, isn't it?"

"Don't be angry," said Abhilash. "See what book I have found, a book on magic mythology. It says that a pixie once shouted so loudly in a demon's ear, that he became half dead. Maybe we can found out the descendant of this pixie?"

"Oh, what a brilliant plan! Go on, Abhilash. No one has stopped you."

"Ok, look at this cage," said Abhilash, nudging Siya to look at another of his randomly picked books. "It says that this had once helped in locking a humangous monster, and saved many people's lives. The monster lost all his powers while inside the cage."

"What the –

The painting on the book suddenly caught her eye. The painting was of blazing white flames, surrounding what Abhilash had just said- a humangous monster. She went through the page for about five more minutes. The next thing Abhilash knew was that his hand had been firmly gripped by a highly thrilled Siya who was shouting, "Mahashakti! Mahashakti!," and was dragging him down the stairs at her fullest speed, her upraised right hand holding the dangling book triumphantly in air.

"Mahashakti," cried out Siya again as she reached the second floor, finally letting go of Abhilash's hand when she saw Rajeshwari walking steadily towards her.

"Look at this, Mahashakti. I think this can really help as a counter attack against Danav," said Siya, panting. Jack and Jenny who had rushed behind her, quite alarmed that she had started running so immediately, were also panting. "At least in a small way, I think. This cage, known as the Kaaragaar cage, had once kept this large monster inside it! A powerful lisam had cast this spell, *agnivadha bhasmah* on this monstrous demon. Many people's lives were saved. Then that lisam cast another death spell, which killed the demon."

"Agnivadha bhasmah. I have never come across this spell," she said thoughtfully. "So this creates the Kaaragar cage," she went on, impressed with the new spell. "That's a very good discovery, kids."

"I found it," said Abhilash. "Credit goes to me."

"We can't kill him, of course," went on Siya. "Killing him would lead to the death of Mahashakti Maheshewari. But at least we can give him a life of prison. At least we can stop the demons from killing innocent pixies, and ragging lisams."

"Then I don't see why we should wait anymore to take our revenge on those bloody devils," said Rajeshwari, her face filled with radiance of determination and a thirst for vengeance. "The decision is made. We will fight them on the very same day, the ninety ninth of 15th October, 2012. I will right away call the Assembly, and make the announcement. If you want to watch, then do so from here. But don't come to the hall. And you know why."

"I know," said Siya.

"How will we watch from here?" asked Abhilash, as Rajeshwari went through the floor to the Assembly Hall, as if the floor was air.

"Like this," said Siya, and she clutched her amulet bearing necklace, closed her eyes and whispered to her bluestone that she wanted to see the happenings of the Assembly Hall on a screen. She knew that simple things like this could work just by the magic of will.

Instantaneously, a screen appeared before them, showing them the Assembly Hall filled with orderly standing lisams, pixies, and rakshaks, (among whom

Udghoshak was the only person whom they recognized), and Rajeshwari walking courteously to the Sinhasan.

"Let's go to my room," suggested Siya. "We will sit there and watch."

Within quarter of a minute, Siya and Abhilash were seated on the comfy pink couches of Siya's pinkish-wallpapered room, where they saw Rajeshwari stand in front of the Sinhasan in a majestic sort of way, motioning the others to sit. Then she spoke.

"Chief Rakshaks and Ministers of Jadooi Jahan! Warriors and Defenders! Judges and Intellectuals! I have got what I had wanted before attacking the demons of Andheri Jahan. Brace yourselves! Because now we are going to fight against Danav and his demons."

This one sentence made the hall roar with enthusiastic and satisfied cries of praise for the Mahashakti, and Jadooi Jahan.

"Don't ask me today that why I have never announced this battle, which I should have done years ago. There's a reason. And once this battle is over, may it be our victory or loss, I will tell you the reason why I had never let this battle happen earlier. The demons have taken innocent lives! They have orphaned our kids and widowed our sisters. They have flowed rivers of blue blood. Now it's time to take revenge."

The hall again rang out with roars of praise for the Mahashakti, and vengeance filled cries for the demons.

"I just have one condition!"

Silence fell over the Assembly Hall.

"No one would touch Danav, because he is my pray. Only, and only my pray. Because I would be casting a special, highly powerful spell on him, right from the beginning. And going near him might harm you, which I do not want to entertain."

The Assembly Hall approved of this.

"So it's final. We are going to fight against them on the very same day, the ninety nineth of 15th October, 2012. I will be sending this message to Danav today. Is there anyone who wants to oppose?"

Undoubtedly, not a soul spoke.

"Any questions?"

The General stepped forward.

"Yes, General?" asked Rajeshwari.

"Nothing about the battle, Mahashakti," he said. "But I wanted to know about our new guests at the palace."

Rajeshwari froze. What does he know about them, she thought worriedly.

"I always note down the purpose of visit in the Royal Maintenance Diary, when outsiders come to the Shakti Bhawan. But when I asked others about these kids, I found out that no one knew about them. They just said that the kids had accompanied you while coming here."

"Oh, thanks God," thought Rajeshwari in relief.

"So if you could just tell me," the General continued, thinking whether he should have asked this silly thing in the Assembly in front of everyone, "what I should write in the maintenance diary, your highness, it would be a great help."

"Oh, the kids. They are from Sunhairi Jahan," lied Rajeshwari. "The girl's name is Siya, my friend- Nisha's daughter. And the boy is Abhilash, a friend of Siya. They wanted to visit our palace, so Nisha sent them here. So just fill that blank with 'tourists' under the purpose column."

"Thankyou, your highness," said the Geneal, and backed off.

"Anything else?" asked Rajeshwari.

Seeing that no one had any objection, she declared "Assembly ends!," and came up to Siya's room hoping that she would be there, and to her luck- she was.

"Did you watch the Assembly?" Rajeshwari asked.

"Yes,Mahashakti," replied Siya. "But I was thinking that- what will we do if Naagin again turns herself into someone else? We could be easily tricked, if she does so!"

"Don't worry about that. Udghoshak has already put the true-comer charm on Shakti Bhawan's entrance gate. If anyone tries to enter our palace in a fake form, he or she would be burned most immediately and the person in no time would return into his original form."

"And Mahashakti, now I remember that when we were in the cave, I mean, in Mayamahal, there was a very very old book. Is there anything special about it? When we made that floral design, the book was what got displayed inside the diamond-shaped rays."

"That book" said Rajeshwari, "is where a person's name is registered when a person goes out of the magical world or steps inside the magical world. Of course, you didn't see your name being written there, but it did get recorded in it."

"Ohh! I see."

"Siya! What are you doing there?" asked Rajeshwari in alarm, shocked that Siya was going to almost touch the spiral bulb at a corner. These spiral bulbs were present in all four corners of the room for decoration. "Come here, come here at once! Do you want to burn yourself and get fainted or what? Stay away from brightness, when the power is so high."

"But I have already gone there and touched it. It didn't do any harm to me," said Siya, surprised at Rajeshwari's worry. "It's just the glow, it's not fire right?"

"Is that another characteristic of humans? You are not allergic to powerful lights?"

"No," said Abhilash in an obvious matter-of-factly voice.

"You mean you don't faint when you get near bright light of even extremely high power?"

"No, we don't," said Siya.

NAAGIN

"Come here, Anika," said Danav, taking her to the central bureau of Andheri Jahan. "I will show you some-

"What is all this, Naagin?" asked Danav horrified as well as infuriated, as he saw on opening the door was a yellowish brown room (which was supposed to be the central bureau) with lightened earthen diyas all over the walls, and a large square shaped hawan kund in the centre of the floor, and Naagin sitting cross legged before the high rising black smoke from the hawan kund, and throwing burnt ash at the hawan kund with closed eyes and muttering mantras, as if some Indian tantrik's ghost had got into her. "Do you think this is your playhouse?"

Anika looked at the ceiling, which had now turned from green to black.

"If I tell you what I have found," said Naagin, slowly opening her eyes. "You will regret that you were ever harsh on me."

"What are you up to?" asked Danav, totally taken aback at Naagin's new discovery.

"This!" she said, as she picked up a black mask with a pair of tongs. "This is what I call a 'killer mask', because once a demon wears this mask, no ordinary shine will be able to stop our demons from killing our enemies."

"Proof?" asked Danav, flatly.

Naagin clapped her hands twice, and a demon came to the room.

"Any order for this servant, master?" he asked. This demon had the face of a fish, and the body of a bear, with claws of a bird.

"Put this on your face," ordered Naagin, handing him a killer mask from the pile of masks that she had crafted till now."

The demon did as he was instructed.

"Prava prasphutita," she pronounced, and a six feet long light bulb appeared at some distance from where they were standing.

"Go and touch that," said Naagin.

The demon started shaking all over his body. The look of terror on his face was indistinguishable, even from behind the mask.

"Go!" Naagin hissed. The fish-faced demon nervously approached the light bulb, relieved that he was not dead yet. His shaking hand slowly rose to touch the light, as Rakshak saw the scene expectantly. The demon finally touched the bulb, and to his utmost surprise, nothing happened to him. He was still alive.

"Now you come here, and give me back that mask," said Naagin. The demon obediently took out the mask, and gave it to Naagin.

"Now go there again," said Naagin. "Believe me, nothing would happen to you."

The demon Asura walked towards the bulb, this time with confidence. But as soon as he went near the bulb, the light of the bulb evaporated him, and he disappeared with an ear-shuddering loud cry. The demon had died.

"Brilliant!" cried out Danav, filled with ecstatic happiness. He went and kissed Naagin on the forehead, and said, "So what are we waiting for? Let's get the throne of Jadooi Jahan."

"I can't wait for the day of my coronation," said Naagin dreamily.

Anika was still surveying the room.

"But why my bureau, Naagin?" asked Danav.

"Because I found out this room to have the highest concentration of dark powers," said Naagin.

"There's a message for you, Lord," a demon Asuri came and reported.

"Message for me?" asked Danav flabbergasted. "Who has sent it?"

"It's from Jadooi Jahan, my Lord," said the Asuri.

"Show me," said Danav, and the parchment unrolled itself and hung in front of Danav.

Respected King of Jadooi Jahan,

This message is to inform you that we want the truthwand back, because it is Jadooi Jahan's property. And if we do not receive the truthwand by tomorrow, we will be left with no choice but to fight against you.

The choice is yours. Either return us the truthwand peacefully, or be ready for the war on the ninety ninth day of 15th October, 2012, on the battleground of Jadooi Jahan.

I shall be waiting for your reply. Write back soon.

Yours sincerely,

Mahashakti Rajeshwari

"Naagin, I think I have a good plan," said Danav thoughtfully.

"What plan?" asked Naagin.

"Today is the 25th day of 15th ocober, 2012. And they have set the date for the 99th day of 15th October, right?

"Yes," said Naagin, "So what are you thinking of?"

"What I am thinking is, let's send the message to Jadooi Jahan that we agree to fight on that date, that is, ninety ninth. But what if we attack them some days before the fixed date, like say, on the Rang Festival? This century, it's on the eighty fourth day of 15th October. If we do so, then the attack would be much before they would have expected. Our demons can get prepared by then, can't they? So, what do you say?

"And we'll have the same advantage like you had the last time," said Naagin. "The people would be busy in enjoying the festival"

"Exactly," said Danav.

"This is the best plan I have ever heard of in my life," said Naagin dreamily. "I already feel like the queen of the world!"

THE TRUTH

It was the eighty second day of 15ᵗʰ October, 2012. Practice for the upcoming war was going explicably well. Everyone was doing their best. Even the common citizens, both men and women, had started training for any defence that they may provide for the family. Contended with her day's learnings, Siya came to bed happy and satisfied, and changed her navy blue gown to a nighty (Siya and Abhilash had started wearing gowns and sherwanis respectively, the type of clothes available in Jadooi Jahan). Sitting on the bed, she pulled the curtains of the door and the window, and started switching off the four spherical light bulbs at the four corners of the room (using instructions, of course).

As she was about to turn off the last bulb, she caught a faint movement of a diffused shadow behind the window curtain. But whatever she had seen suddenly vanished. She got out of her bed and went a little further to look closely at the window, searching for signs of any more movement or a glimpse of some shadow. She simply stared at the window for about two minute. She thought of opening the window and checking out if there was something, but then she felt stupid, and went back to the bed. She switched off the final bulb, and decided to sleep.

She had just lied down when the window's glass opened with an audible *krrr,* making her jump.

"What's happening?" Siya groaned irritably, and then focused her eyes on the intruder who had just entered her room through the window.

"You? What are you doing here?" she said with a mixture of surprise and fury and grief surging up her throat, all at the same time. For the person who stood before her was none other than Anika, her ex-best friend, in a green gown that symbolized her to be close with demons.

"I'll explain," began Anika frantically. "See, what happened is –

"Go away from here!" yelled Siya, her brain jammed with inexpressible sorrow. "If you want to be alive, then just get lost. Fly away to your master's fairyland."

"Siya, I –

"Please don't talk to me for goodness's sake, Anika. The last person I would have expected to turn against me was you."

"Siya let me explain –

"What is there left to explain? How could you do this to me, Anika? Just how could you? How could you betray me? I don't know in which way I should tell you how much I trusted you. I..I.. just don't know what to tell you. You just –

"SIYA, LISTEN TO ME!" burst out Anika, suddenly losing her temper. "Just shut up for a moment and listen to me, will you? I thought we were best friends! I thought that the word betrayal didn't exist in the dictionary of our friendship."

"Yes, it didn't," said Siya in a diminished voice. "But now it's there. YOU ADDED IT!" She was yelling again.

"Siya! How can you say that? What has happened to you?"

"Just get away from here, Anika," said Siya, grabbing a sword from the wall and placing it at Anika's throat. "Get away from here this very minute, or else I will simply behead you with this sword," said Siya with as much hatred in her tone as she could bring up.

"Go on, then," said Anika flatly, feeling speechless. "I anyways don't want to live a life where even my best friend isn't ready to listen why I had to pretend that I hated her," she said, fighting away tears that had started to form beneath her eyes.

"You were pretending?" asked Siya in shock. The sword fell down from her hand and hit the ground with a loud thud. "Why on earth were you pretending to hate me?"

"Certainly I wasn't doing all this just for pleasure, Siya," said Anika, holding back a sob. "They were going to kill you! And they had the Kaala Jal. I didn't know when they wanted to kill you. All I knew was that there was a chance of your life being saved if I pretended to be your arch enemy. What do you think I would get if Danav wins or you die?"

"But all that you told them outside the floating house where I was kept," said Siya, feeling so guilty that she wanted to die. "I couldn't believe...I just...I don't know... it was like...I felt so sad, so hurt."

They just gazed at each other, with aching hearts, tear filled eyes, for what seemed like hours, though it was just a minute. They didn't know what to speak. None of them could find a way to break this awkward silence.

Then Siya braved to speak. "So, friends again?" she asked, stretching her hand towards Anika.

"I had never broken this friendship. It was you who didn't have the faith," said Anika painfully.

"Oh Anika!" Siya cried as she flung her arms around Anika. "I'm so sorry."

"It's okay," said Anika, hugging her back. "I know you would never disbelieve me the second time," she said, now letting a sea of tears flow down her eyes uncontrollably.

"See. I don't have a lot of time," she said all of a sudden, wiping away her tears and sounding all business-like. "So you just listen to me."

Siya gave a swift nod, rubbing her eyes and face to make it non tear-strained.

"The Rang Festival is just two days far," said Anika, now sounding like a warning newspaper report. "And they are preparing to attack you on Rang Festival, they think that the lisams and the pixies will be engrossed in enjoying the colours, and their way to the fall of Amarshikha will be clear."

"But the demons are allergic to light…" began Siya.

"And Naagin has created killer masks, which are light repellents," Anika cut in. "That's the only reason for which Danav is so longingly looking forward to this war."

"Light repellents!" Siya thought, and gasped with horror.

"And this Pavitra Pushpa which they have; God knows where they hide it after its use. Danav has completely exhausted the flower. He orders it every day to build demons of a variety of species, and tires it to produce more and more until it withers for the day. The numbers of demons he has made through it are huge in number, almost about one lakh!"

"Oh dear God!" moaned Siya. "They're ruining the Pavitra Pushpa."

"Okay, now the most important thing!" she said, taking out a small black glassed bottle. "It's the Kaala jal, the black water. It's more than poison. Just one drop of this can kill you in a fraction of seconds. Mahashakti Mahaeshwari had summoned this to kill Danav. Now Danav wants to kill you in the same way in which Mahashakti Mahashwari had attempted to kill him."

"But how did you get this?"

"Stole it," said Anika. "It of course won't be helpful to kill Danav, as killing him would mean killing Mahashakti Mahashwari too. But it can come in handy to kill some other demons."

"You are a genius!" Siya exclaimed. "I'm sure it must be very difficult to reach."

"It was. Well, a bit of eavesdropping and a little bit of trust did the work to know the location. It was in the central bureau, which is now a havan kund room for Naagin to make killer masks. The Kaala Jal was in a red glass case, protected by a password. But it didn't take much time to crack it. Thanks to *criminal case*, the video game today saved your life."

"And have you gathered any clues for the whereabouts of the Pavitra Pushpa?"

"Unfortunately not," said Anika in a remorseful voice.

"Well you could hack the Kaala Jal. That was no easy task."

"I wish I could mix this Kaala Jal in their food or drink. Pity that when people are in this land, they don't feel hungry or thirsty, and get all the energy just by breathing."

"I know, right? The work would turn so much simpler."

"Well, what was Abhilash doing in Andheri Jahan? He made me rub my eyes twice and pinch myself thrice to be sure that he was here."

"The idiot followed us," replied Siya. "God knows why"

"Oh! So it was him all the way down to your home who gave me the goosebumps kind of feeling that someone was following me. And I think that's why you felt something funny about the golden bush, he must be there hiding behind it all the time."

"Yeah, right!" said Siya, narrowing her eyes. "And probably it was him in the cave also. Remember? When things fell down, and we thought that it must be the cat."

"Yeah!" said Anika. "Okay, drop it. Now tell me what I should do. Should I go back to Andheri Jahan and continue to pretend how much I loathe you, or should I stay here?"

"I don't want you to go, you know. It's dangerous there," said Siya. "What do you think?"

"I want you to do the thinking part," said Anika. "I hate making choices."

"Okay, I have an idea," said Siya.

"Tell me the idea," said Anika, as she saw Siya close her eyes and clutch the bluestone hanging from her necklace, and then mutter something that she couldn't make out.

"Hey, I like your necklace," complimented Anika.

"Thanks!" said Siya with a smile, as an exact copy of the black glass bottle containing the Kaala Jal appeared on her hand. "I made it in that dim floating house of Andheri Jahan."

"That bottle looks exactly like this one!," exclaimed Anika. "I see you have learnt a good bit of magic here"

"I had to," said Siya. "So my idea is that: you take this fake black glass bottle with seveneering essence, and keep it in place of the Kaala Jal."

"Wow! That's a superb plan," said Anika happily. "Siya, I think I should leave now. I don't want Danav to find out that I had come here to reveal his secrets to you."

"Okay. But how will you go?," asked Siya.

"Just the way I had come here," replied Anika. "By flying. Danav gave me this black feather, so that I can come to his office and keep a record of all the details for the weapons, killing masks, and all sorts of other things related to the war. He likes my handwriting, and makes me write all day like a slave."

"Okay, now go," insisted Siya, nudging her to leave. "But be very careful. And keep this star with you," she said, presenting a crystalline five pointed star to Anika. "Mahashakti had given this to me. It's a protector kind of thing, shaped like the sign of Jadooi Jahan. Whenever you are in a problem, clutch this star tightly in your hand. As I have presented this to you, I will automatically know that you are in trouble. My bluestone will turn green, and start throbbing."

"Thanks Siya," Anika hugged her, and said "Bye," as she took out her grey feather and flew out of the window, into the blue sky, and high above into the darkness of Andheri Jahan.

REPLACEMENT

After placing the fake glass bottle of seveneering essence in the central bureau, Anika slowly flew to the maroon floating house allotted to her by Naagin. She slowly crept through the edge of the floating building to her room, making sure that no one was awake to see her and blessing her luck that she had replaced the Kaala Jal with the seveneering essence almost as easily as she had taken it out from the red glass case, which was just by mouthing the password 'poison'.

She silently opened the door and rapidly bolted it, taking a sigh of relief. Just the moment Anika turned around, what she found in front of her was Danav glaring at her, already inside the room.

"I thought you wouldn't mind if I asked where you were when everyone else was sleeping," said Danav.

"Me? I –

"Yes you!," barked Danav. "What were you doing out of your room when you ought to be sleeping?"

"Nothing. I was just roaming around," said Anika, trying to sound as confident as she could, though she couldn't make her heartbeat pound slower, no matter however much she tried to calm down.

"Why?" Danav asked coldly.

"Loneliness," she said suddenly, wondering how and why that word had come out. "Yeah, I felt lonely. Very lonely," she tried to give logical explanations for the word that her brain had just ordered her mouth to speak. "I miss my brother. I miss my home," she continued extending her explanation. "Whenever I feel sad, I generally go out for a short walk, or a bicycle ride. It helps me feel happy."

"I will be keeping my eyes on you," hissed Danav, making Anika feel very uncomfortable, and stalked out of the room.

Anika crawled into her bed, exhausted. She wanted to worry about a thousand things, but fell asleep as soon as she closed her eyes.

RANG FESTIVAL

Rang Festival came soon. Siya raised her head from a pink quill, and sat up in her round white bed, the only non-pink material in the room. She had informed Mahashakti and Udghoshak about Anika's truth, and all the information that she had given, shown them the Kaala Jal that she had brought for them, and taunted Abhilash that following Anika at late night was not respectable at all.

Everything was ready now. Rajeshwari had sent announcements in all zones of Jadooi Jahan that they were going to be attacked on the Rang Festival, and therefore all of them should be armed, headstrong, and prepared to face the situation, even the common citizens. The practise of the Rakshak lisams and pixies had increased fourfold. The strength of the army was growing, both in quality and quantity. Even the wild creatures, who were part of the rakshak army, had summoned many other non-rakshak creatures to get included in the army.

Rajeshwari, Siya and Abilash had spent their whole days learning and applying new spells. Siya had even suggested to use the most deadly weapon on earth: guns and bullets in place of ancient arrows, swords and spears. But unfortunately, no summoning or transforming charm could bring them these. Udghoshak was keeping records of each and every detail necessary for the war, and carrying out regular checks on various places for any sign of demon spies. Overall, Jadooi Jahan was prepared.

Siya came out of her bed and looked out of the window at the blue sky. Just as Mahashkti Rajeshwari had described, she saw that the white fluffy clouds were now showering vibrant bubbles, which burst out into dust colours and water colours upon descending on something or someone below. Some lisams even managed to get hold of the colours in their bubble form, and splashed it on someone else with great vigour and laughter. The Amarshikha on the Shakti Stupa was glowing as magnificently as ever. She did not want its glow to be extinguished. She did not want Jadooi Jahan to drown in the darkness of Danav's selfish ambitions. She did not want this Rang Festival to be the last.

"Siya!" called someone, interrupting her worries. She looked around to see that it was Abhilash. "MS is calling us," he said.

"To her room?" Siya asked.

"No. She is downstairs," said Abhilash. "Near the Assembly Hall."

"Okay." They moved down through the glass, and saw Rajeshwari moving from one place to another, just as she did whenever she was worried.

"Siya! Abilash! Well, first of all, Happy Rang!" said Rajeshwari, finally stopping at one place.

"Yeah, Happy Rang!," said Abhilash to Rajeshwari, and then to Siya with a gleeful smile, shaking hands with her.

"Same to you," she said, returning back a glowing smile to Abhilash. "And Happy Rang to you as well, Mahashakti. Many many happy returns of the day!"

"Thank you!" said Rajeshwasri, smiling at Siya and Abhilash, and then came to a serious mood. "And secondly, I called you for telling all the precautions one last time. Siya, you will try to stay away from Danav, because his main aim is you. Abhilash, revise the spells. Remember, they will be your greatest weapon," she said the last two words with emphasis. "Do you two have your swords all polished and sharpened?"

They showed her their shiny swords.

"Are your feathers working?"

They flew on their feathers, which were working perfectly alright.

"Siya, do you have the Kaala Jal safely with you?" Rajeshwari asked.

"Yes, Mahashakti," said Siya, showing her the black glass case containing the black water.

"Maahi had made this to fight back irresistible demons, but I had never thought till the age of twelve that we would ever face a situation where we will need this," said Rajeshwari, becoming a bit sentimental. And again in an instant, she revived her enthusiastic self, and advised, "Use the Kaala Jal only for powerful opponents, like Naagin or the demon general or Surasura, or maybe Kaali Trishna. Don't waste it on demons. Use the fire spell on them, it will easily kill them.

"They can't wave fire spells on us, that's lucky for us. As you know that demons mostly don't know how to cast spells, they will mostly attack by spears and swords. Whenever you think that it's not easy to kill the demon trying to attack you, use the spell - *trahi mam.* Always remember that it's more important to save yourself than to kill your enemy. But if you face any major demon, then apply your brains and think which spell would be appropriate at that moment.

"I have told everyone to act as if they don't know anything. Their demons are about one lakh, and our rakshaks just twenty thousand. Oh yes, now it has increased to twenty five thousand. But our rakshaks are more efficient, and they know more than just working spears and swords. They know how to cast spells, and they know how to defend themselves and others. If God wishes, then we will save Jadooi Jahan, and the greatest demon on earth would be in our capture.

"Well, the demons can be attacking any moment. So be careful, and be ready."

"Yeah," said Siya.

"Good luck," said Rajeshwari and left. Siya had just began revising the spells in her mind, when she suddenly felt a throbbing sensation against her chest. As she looked down at her bluestone, she saw that the blue-coloured amulet had now turned green.

"Abhilash!" said Siya in panic. "Anika is in danger!"

"What? How do you know?"

"My bluestone has turned green. Look!" she said, showing him what was now a greenstone.

"So what will we do now? Tell MS?" asked Abhilash.

"No, she is busy. She is giving instructions to the rakshaks."

"CAN I HELP IN ANY WAY?" came a deep ruffled voice, which was unmistakably Udghoshak's.

"Udghoshak! I…that…Anika…she is.." fumbled Siya.

"I KNOW," said Udghoshak. *"I HEARD YOU. SIYA, DON'T PANIC. JUST KEEP CALM AND CONCENTRATE ON HOW YOU WILL FIGHT THE WAR. LEAVE ANIKA'S WORRY TO ME. I WILL GO THERE AND TRY TO RESCUE HER. YOU GO DOWN AND ENJOY THE RANG FESTIVAL UNTIL THE DEMONS ARRIVE. THE COLOURS WILL HELP TO WIPE AWAY YOUR FEARS. HAPPY RANG!"* Saying so, he rolled himself and fluttered away.

"Happy Rang!" Siya waved back. Please be safe Anika, she thought. Please don't let anything bad happen to you. You had saved my life. If anything happens to you, Anika…I will never be able to forgive myself. Never…

WHEN DEMONS ATTACK

"Throw more salt," Danav snapped, lashing Anika with a whip like a beast.

Submissively, two Asuris threw handfuls of salt at a bleeding Anika, her clothes now in tatters with Danav's whips, her blood spotted hands tied to silver chains hanging from the ceiling of a dark dungeon, her drooping face smeared with dust and blood, the unbearable pain making her almost unconscious.

"What did you think? You will steal my Kaala Jal and I won't even know? It was very clever to pretend to be your best friend's foe. But it was extremely foolish to think that replacing the Kaala Jal with seveneering essence was a clever idea to fool me." Rakshak gave Anika another cruel blow with the whip, making her moan agonizingly. "I will not leave you. I will whip you to death. And your death would be so painful that you will regret that you had ever met Siya."

"You can kill me, Danav. But you can't do anything to Siya," she said weakly, and yet ferociously. "She is destined to destroy you, Danav. You will be killed by her."

"Shut up!" Danav cried out dangerously, whipping Anika even more hard. But this time, Anika smiled at the pain and said, "Whip me as much as you can, Danav. Lash me as long as you are alive."

"HAAH," cried Danav going crazy with anger, and lashed Anika as brutally as he could, making his own hand bleed.

"You still have time, Danav," said Anika, trying to stop herself from fainting. "Change your decision and make a wise choice. Return the truthwand back to Mahashakti Rajeshwari, and ask for forgiveness. Mahashakti is very kind, she will forgive you."

"NO!" roared Danav thunderously. "NO!" he yelled again. "You have so much of faith in your friend's power, don't you? I will break your faith. I will break your pride and ego. I want to kill you right now. But I won't. I will first give death to Siya, I will teach her what it means go against me. I will drop her corpse in front of your eyes. And then I will kill you."

He kicked Anika on her waist, making her lose control, as a consequence of which her lips hit the left silver chain and started bleeding as the rest of her body.

Throwing the whip at an Asura, Danav scowled at the unconscious Anika. He put on his black killer mask and grabbed his deathwand. He came out of the floating house, and saw Naagin waiting for him with all his demons ready for the war, with their killing masks on their faces. He grinned maliciously and shouted, "Head to Jadooi Jahan!"

At this one order, everyone turned their bodies upside down and dived towards The Great Black, and down into the brightness of Jadooi Jahan.

Looking at the huge horde of both handsome and ugly demons (some of them even looked like innocent humans), the General yelled, "They have come! ARM YOURSELVES!"

Without a single second of delay, the brave rakshaks of Jadooi Jahan had abandoned their pretendence of enjoying the Rang Festival and started focusing aims at the enemies. And within a few minutes, the play of colours had changed into the play of weapons. Sensing the people's lack of enthusiasm, the clouds stopped releasing colourful bubbles and sadly disappeared.

Danav looked gladly at his one lakh demons easily demolishing the struggling rakshaks, who were clearly much lesser in number. The air of Jadooi Jahan was rented with shouts like -

"Rakshaks, Attack!"

"Demons, Kill them!"

"Target straight on their masks!"

"Leave the arrows on the call of three"

"Demons, shield your faces!"

"Rakshaks! Take your positions!"

Werewolves were biting and tearing away creatures that looked like a combination of dogs and octopus. Flying unicorns were neighing and kicking ferociously at limping zombies. Huge butterflies were casting spells at ghouls. Two three giant mammothosorauses with horns like barasingha attacked ten demons at a time. Apsaras were slaying attractive Asuris.

Siya and Abhilash casted fire spells at any demon who came in their way, as they witnessed a savage war that they would not have imagined in the worst of their nightmares. An intense fight of swords was going on between the General and Surasura. Naagin, who had turned into her original form of reptilady: a giant snake, was now spitting green venoms here and there, converting herself into a woman after the exhaustion of killing three to four people, and again reviving into her perilous serpentine figure after a good rest. Arrows flew from one side to another. Blue blood and shouts of cries of death and pain could be seen and heard respectively from every corner.

Danav, eager to commit some delightful murders himself, raised his hands to cast death spells at a group of Rakshaks. But to his amazement, his hands got stuck as he saw flames of white form around him. In front of him was Rajeshwari glaring at him revengefully. One step forward made his fingers catch fire, making him jump with pain. Rajeshwari saw him use a fire-defence charm to stop his hands from burning, and flew away with satisfaction that the main demon was now in their captive.

"What have you put around me?" screamed Danav after her, and frantically kept turning in circles. He shrieked and bellowed for help, but no one of his demons, not even Naagin could find out a way to rescue him out of the Kaaragar cage.

Siya put another fire spell at a five headed dark brown bat with gnarled teeth that disappeared with a 'hmmrrrahh'. Then she noticed a small furred pixie flying towards a headless skeleton, and killing it bravely with a knife sized sword. Then the little pixie turned to attack a vampire woman with two long tails, and Siya recognised the pixie at once – Jack, her guard pixie. She smiled happily as Jack fearlessly approached towards the vampire. But just when the vampire had stretched her long pointed fingernails to defend Jack's sharp sword, a handsome demon from behind pushed his knife through

Jack's furry stomach, and he fell dead on the ground in a pool of his own blue blood.

Siya gasped in anguish, as she flew down to bandage Jack and carry him to her room. But when she came down and checked his heartbeat, she realized that he was not breathing.

"Jack!," she whispered in his ear with a shock. "Jack, wake up! Jack!" she cried. But Jack gave no response. Jack was never going to wake up, she thought bitterly. "Jack, why did this happen to you?" she cried, as she hugged the dead little blue-furred pixie to her bosom. She became so traumatised at the death of Jack that she didn't even notice that she was now gathered by six demons, until a spear came flying at her from somewhere else, and she shouted, 'Trahi mam!'. This made all six demons fall back and the spear stop on its track, and Siya cast a death spell on them so ferociously that all six of the demons vanished with great cries of 'vroooohhhh' and 'hmmmrrraahhh'.

"So you are the messiah," said a woman's voice from behind. Siya turned around to see a pretty woman with long black hair and extensive black feathers, dressed in a black ball gown – a total contrast to her skin which was entirely white. "You are Siya, aren't you?" she asked.

"Yes, I am," said Siya, thinking who this woman was, as she got pulled to gaze at her sparkling black eyeballs.

"Hi, I am Kaali. Kaali Trishna. If I present your dead body to Danav, he will be impressed with me, and he will give me what I deserve, what Naagin has snatched from me. In place of Naagin, I will be the queen of the magical world, I will be his ladylove, and I will be known as the most beautiful lady of the universe. Only I."

"Yeah, you will," said Siya, struggling to free herself from getting hypnotized by the attractive stare of Kaali's black eyes. "So go and get rid of Naagin. Leave me."

"Not so easily," said Kaali softly with a smile.

"Leave me at once, or else I will cast the fire spell at you!" shouted Siya, trying her best to cut the eye contact with Kaali's black eyes.

"First look around you, and then speak," said Kaali, still smiling. "Take a single step back or forward, and you will only aid to kill yourself faster."

Siya looked around herself, finally getting rid of Kaali's eyes. It was now that she grasped the fact that Kaali's exceptionally long feathers had trapped around her like a rope, just as a python would do before swallowing its prey. She tried all her best to stand still at one place, as Kaali's eerily long black feathers wrapped fiercely around her body. The grasp of the feathers became tighter and tighter, making it impossible to breathe. More feathers rose from Kaali and wrapped themselves as a double coat around Siya's ankle, then the knees, and now tightening on her chest. Not knowing which spell to use, she stiffly freed her hands with a lot of twisting and turning of wrists, and took out the Kaala Jal - her last choice.

"W-Wh-What's that?" asked Kaali, finally taking out the irritating gorgeous smile from her face, as a final feather began forming around Siya's neck.

"You will know," said Siya, as she poured a drop of Kaala Jal on her face. Immediately her face and then her body became as black as her black eyeballs, and she was dead and gone without revealing a single noise of pain or fury.

The next thing that Siya heard was the General shouting - "Form the Chakravyuh! Quick! CHAKRAVYUH!" With an excellent sword movement, he sliced Surasura dead and flew up towards the Shakti Stupa with his yellow feather.

"PROTECT THE AMARSHIKHA!" cried a Rakshak cheetah with mauveine-coloured zebra stripes, as a swarm of eighty thousand demons(the others were dead by now) proceeded towards the Shakti Stupa(though none of them dared to come closer than fifteen metres of its reach) and shooted arrows and spears at the Amarshikha, trying to compel it to fall on the ground and get extinguished.

Within a split second, the left fifteen thousand rakshaks formed a large protective circle of Chakravyuh around the Amarshikha, though they too maintained a distance of eight metres from the the star's scorching glow.

Rajeshwari and Abhilash below were preventing Naagin from destroying the Kaaragar cage to free Danav, who had almost become successful in cancelling the cage's flames a minute ago, which Rajeshwari had very difficultly cast again to its power.

The demons ruthlessly threw spears and spiny stones at the Amarshikha, some weapons which escaped through the Chakravyuh and hit the Amarshikha, some which injured the rakshaks, and some which were hit back by the rakshaks' weapons.

Siya saw helplessly as arrows and spades flew to the Amarshikha. Now the glowing star shaped shine had moved by some distance to the right from its stand. Now another strong arrow or large stone would have made the star fall from the tower. She saw the demon archers take focus to leave another bunch of arrows, as the rakshaks tried to strengthen their chakravyuh and defend the Amarshikha with all their might.

Without thinking anything, Siya directly flew towards the Amarshikha and raised the glowing star from its position as a hundred arrows about to strike it hit each other and vanished. What happened next made everyone watch Siya with spellbound wonder, as this was something which had never happened before in the history of Jadooi Jahan.

Even the bravest of the brave would not have have dared to do what Siya had just done. She had not only gone near the Amarshikha and touched it, but also raised it high above her head even though she had started burning. Anyone else would have died in a second upon the slightest touch of the Amarshikha. But Siya, burning painfully within the halo of flames, was still alive, taking the last of her few breaths.

As soon as Siya raised the shimmering star above her head, in an attempt to take it away from the arrows, the white flying feather in her left hand burnt and vanished, and her bluestone emitted a narrow beam of blue ray upwards at the upper tip of Amarshikha.

"Siya! STOP!" cried Rajeshwari, flying up to the Shakti Stupa. But she was still very far from the tower when she saw the rays of every zone's shine getting focused at the tip of the Amarshikha. She weakly watched at the sky, as Siya, not able to tolerate the blazing heat anymore, burnt down into ashes. As a consequence of the merging of the bright rays from all shines of Jadooi Jahan, there was an outblast of red fire. Rakshaks and demons backed away in fear of their lives. They still couldn't believe how a small girl had so much of courage to save the Amarshikha without thinking of her own life's safety. The erosion of the red fire melted all the demons to death, despite the killer masks, and even injured some rakshaks.

Today, the sacrifice of one life had saved the lives of thousands of rakshaks, and killed all the demons in one go. The Amarshikha had returned to its dignified position over the Shakti Stupa. "This girl cannot be an ordinary lisam," said a pixie. This is what all the rakshaks, and all the citizens who had seen the view felt – *'This girl is not an ordinary lisam.'*

THE FINAL WAR

Abhilash came running to the spot below the Amarshikha. The ashes of Siya and her necklace fell down before him. The bluestone was somehow unaffected. The ashes assembled themselves into the empty space within the bluestone. Abhilash picked up the necklace, and wore it as a bracelet around his hand. He wanted to cry, but tears didn't come out. Rajeshwari descended down, transfixed at what she had just seen. She had lost another close one, and was again unable to do anything. She was a failure, she thought, 'A complete failure'.

"You are a failure," said someone behind her in agreement with Rajeshwari's thoughts. She turned around, and saw two people smiling evilly at her. The two people were Naagin and Danav, the only supporters of Andheri Jahan left alive. Undoubtedly, Naagin had finally poisoned the Kaaragar cage to its destruction, and Danav had broken out.

"You will HAVE TO pay for it!" she cried out, as all the rakshaks ran towards Danav dangerously, ready to finish him away.

"STOP THERE!" she shouted at the angry rakshaks, who hesitantly stopped running and flying. "Danav is my victim. I will decide what has to be done with him." Danav and Rajeshwari got into a severe conflict, as Naagin in her giant serpentine figure sprang at the roaring rakshaks, who were filled with questions of 'but's and 'why's. To the surprise of Danav and Naagin and Rajeshwari herself, she called Naagin in the middle of the fight between her and Danav. Naagin thought whether she should go or not. But when Rajeshwari angrily snapped at Danav, "Tell your girlfriend to come here if you are not afraid of me," she rushed towards them, though she didn't turn into her woman form. Rajeshwari focused her hand towards Naagin, and immediately cast a spell - *'Obey or freeze'* at her before Danav could stop her.

"What did you cast at her?" asked Danav, not getting the spell that Rajeshwari had uttered. Naagin looked puzzled, at the same state of unawareness as Danav.

"I have put the conditioned freezing charm on the love of your life," replied Rajeshwari. "If you don't handover your wand to me within the count of ten, then the spell will explode and Naagin would freeze to death." The rakshaks watched happily, cheering the brilliant plan of their Mahashakti.

"Well, then there's nothing to think in this," said Danav. "Of course, I will –

'Of course, he will give you the wand right now," said Naagin in an obvious sort of way, without the slightest of fear noticeable in her voice. "He will do anything for me, won't you, love? Just the way I have played over my life just to make you pleased? Give the wand to Siya, Danav. Give it to this filthy lisam," she said calmly, not the least afraid of losing her life.

"Your time" said Rajeshwari sternly, hoping that this time Naagin will not have any clever idea to crush the spell. "starts now! Ten.."

"You are mistaken, Rajeshwari," said Danav flatly. "The love of my life is not a sheer reptilady. My life's love is the throne of Jadooi Jahan."

"Eight...seven..," Rajeshwari counted down the seconds.

"What are you talking of?" asked Naagin, now in a quivering voice of surprise and disgust. She turned herself into a woman, possibly to please Danav with her attractive looks.

"..five..." Rajeshwari continued the countdown.

"Then let her die," said Danav, hardly showing any emotion. "I don't care."

"..four.."

"Give her the wand, Danav. NOW!" hissed Naagin furiously.

"..three..two.." went on Rajeshwari.

"Please don't let me die!" Naagin had now kneeled at Danav's feet, pleading him hysterically.

"One.." said Rajeshwari, surprised that Danav had still not done anything to try to save Naagin. The rakshaks held their breaths, as they prayed for Danav to handover the deathwand to the Mahashakti.

"Aaaahhhhh!" cried Naagin, as she turned into her original form - a huge snake, and on the spot froze to death.

"..zero" the countdown finished, and the gigantic frozen statue of the snake fell to the ground with a thud, breaking down into a thousand fragments of ice.

"No!" gasped Rajeshwari. "How could you do this to her? You called her your ladylove, right? You loved her, didn't you?"

"Love is blind, Rajeshwari. I don't live in blindness," said Rakshas, what in his language was called – honesty, and gave an evil, high-pitched, ear piercing laugh.

"I knew that you are heartless. I knew you have a heart of stone. But at least for Naagin…" Rajeshwari trailed off her sentence, not able to believe this much of cruelty. "She had done so much for you, and you don't even regret this! What sort of a person are you?

"I am not a person! I'm a demon!" he said as coldly as ever. "But by killing my Naagin, you have done me a great loss. She was very useful. Starting from her beautiful slim and slimy body to her amazing brain, all of it pleased my nerves. But you took her away from me. And this spell is therefore in the name of Naagin - *Maranam!*" Danav cast a death spell at Rajeshwari with his deathwand, as the hideous skeleton hand on the wand vented shafts of green and red light towards Rajeshwari. *"Trahi Mam!"* she cried in her defence, not knowing any other way to escape this spell. *"Trahi Mam!"* she cried again, but the glistening red and green shafts of light didn't stop or vanish.

Then quite much to Danav's horror, he cried to someone inside him. "No! Stop! You know that coming out from my capture would kill you within a fraction of seconds."

"And so would it do to you," said the voice of a woman, who struggled to come outside from Danav, as

Danav tried to push her inside. "I won't let you touch my sister!," she snapped.

"Maahi!" screamed Rajeshwari, recognizing her sister at once. "No Maahi, don't do this!" she pleaded on bended knees, not caring that the radiating green and red shafts had now reached her and were spreading slowly through the outline of her body, not caring that she was going to die within a few seconds. "Maahi, please don't come out. I have already lost Siya. I have already lost many of my valiant rakshaks. At least you don't go away. PLEASE!"

"Maheshwari, do what your sister is saying," said Danav, as the red and green shafts made Rajeshwari breathless, making her heart pound slower and slower. "DON'T!" cried Danav, as Maheshwari forced herself out of him with an irresistible energy. What Rajeshwari saw next was the deadly red and green light disappearing from around her, and so also her breathlessness, and Danav exploding with a blast as Maheshwari tore out from within him. She gave Rajeshwari a warm smile, and then she too lost her life and fell on the white tile of Shakti Bhawan, staining it blue with the blood oozing out of her head.

The rakshaks watched all this sorrowfully, not being able to understand what had just happened before their eyes. Some of them were able to realize the untold story of the Rang Festival that had occurred thirteen hundred years ago. Some others thought that they had seen the ghost spirit of their previous Mahashakti - Mahashakti Maheshwsari. Jadooi Jahan did not know whether to rejoice over the death of Danav - a demon who had compelled them to die hundred deaths before dying, or to moan over the loss of Siya - a young teenage girl, claiming to come from Sunhairi Jahan, who had sacrificed her life to save the Amarshikha from falling on the ground and getting extinguished. Jadooi Jahan was in a state of bewilderment; for they didn't know whether to celebrate the end of demon rule, or to cry over the actual death of Mahashakti Maheshwari.

Rajeshwari was crying with her head laid on Maheshwari's chest. Abhilash, who was quite disturbed by Siya's death, now came near Rajeshwari and sat beside her.

"Don't cry, Mahashakti," Rajeshwari heard someone say from behind, as a soft hand touched her shoulder. Rajeshwari turned around to see a girl, whom she couldn't recall immediately. But she felt that she had seen this girl somewhere.

"Anika! Udghoshak!" said Abhilash. "Siya…" he stopped, not wanting to utter the word 'died'.

"Oh, so you are Siya's best friend," said Rajeshwari, forcing a smile, as she wiped away her tears. "I am –

"Mahashakti Rajeshwari, I know," said Anika, cutting off Rajeshwari midway. "A pleasure to meet you," she said, stretching her hand towards the Queen.

"Siya exactly behaved this way," said Rajeshwari, shaking hands with Anika. "But you will be pained to know that just like my sister…your friend is no more."

"No!" said Anika, putting her hands on Rajeshwari's lips. "Nothing has happened to them," said Anika, as if giving a statement and not praying for a wish. "Udghoshak not only found and medicated me, but also found the Pavitra Pushpa."

"Oh yes, the Pavitra Pushpa!" exclaimed Rajeshwari, suddenly brightening up. "I had totally forgotten about that."

"It was in my room itself, a place where I would have never searched it," said Anika, and Udghoshak opened a treasure box from where came out a large trunk-sized pink lotus flower. The only difference that made it a non-lotus was two white petals emerging from its base. These two petals were a bit more large then the other pink flowers.

"Where's Siya?" asked Anika impatiently.

"In this," said Abhilash, removing the bluestone necklace from his wrist. "She lifted the Amarshikha to save its glow from fading and dying away. And in the process, she burnt herself." He untied the thread knots, and took out the bluestone from the thread and gave it to Anika. "She burnt down into ashes that broke themselves into tiny dust particles. These particles then got into this bluestone."

Rajeshwari carried Maheshwari near the Pavitra Pushpa and touched her hand to the white petal on one side, and on the other white petal on the opposite side lay the bluestone of Siya. Everyone watched eagerly, as the white petals rolled themselves around the bluestone and Maheshwari's hand. When the divine petals unrolled, the bluestone was sparkling with blue light and Maheshwari's hand was shining with a golden glow.

In the next minute, people were roaring with ecstatic joy and shouting in praise of Mahashakti Maheshwari and Siya, Maheshwari was kissing Rajeshwari on her forehead, Siya, Anika and Abhilash were hugging each other, Pavitra Pushpa had gone back into the treasure box, and Udghoshak was doing a little dance in the air.

Abhilash was the one to speak first after the return of Siya and Maheshwari. "Now she will be the Mahashakti," he said to Rajeshwari pointing his finger towards her elder sister. "So what will I call you? I don't want to change your nickname," asked Abhilash.

"Then don't change it. Let her name be MS. And as for me, you can call me big MS," said Maheshwari with a laugh.

"Big MS, that's supercool," said Abhilash.

"Okay kids, I think that now you should go back to your homes," said Maheshwari. "Udghoshak will take you to Mayamahal, open the door to Siya's storeroom and you all will head straight to your homes."

The three nodded, and gave final hugs to Rajeshwari and Maheshwari.

"And Siya!" called Maheshwari, when they had started to leave for Mayamahal. "Take this bluestone with you," she said, giving Siya the bluestone made back into a necklace, which she had forgotten near the Pavitra Pushpa.

"Oh, thankyou!" said Siya.

"Always keep this with yourself," she said. "Whenever you wish to meet me or Rani, just tell that to this amulet. And I will come near you."

"Really?" asked Siya, her eyes filled with excitement. "Will it do magic on earth also?"

"Yes," said Maheshwari.

"Can I keep my orb too?" asked Abhilash.

"Has anyone asked it back from you?" asked Rajeshwari with a smile.

"Yes!" Abhilash cried blissfully.

"But you won't use it in a wrong way," warned Rajeshwari to the children. "As for you Anika, that star which Siya gave you will work the same way as an amulet."

"You mean I can do magic too?" asked Anika gleefully. "Thanks! Even I will make a necklace with it."

"But it has no holes," reminded Abhilash.

"You will have the best of both worlds," she whispered in Siya's ear, pulling her into an embrace. Siya as well flung her arms around Maheshwari, and gave her a tiny kiss on her cheek.

"I will miss you," said she.

"I will miss you too, baby," said Maheshwari, as Siya gave a last wave of goodbye to Jadooi Jahan and whooshed in the air with Anika, Abhilash and Udghoshak to Mayamahal.

On the way, Siya announced "Now friends, listen to me. No one tells about this to anyone. It's a secret. Agree?" She stretched her hands in front of them, waiting for their reaction.

"I am with you. I won't tell about this to anyone." Saying so, Anika slammed her hand on Siya's.

"Me too." Abhilash gave his approval with a loud thud on the girls' fingers, making them scowl at him and wobble their fingers with 'aaah' and 'ouch'.

"Well abhilash, how did you follow us to the healing pond?" asked Anika. "You couldn't just have walked till there, could you?"

"I did what Udghoshak did," said Abhilash. "I just said 'flying feather', and a scarlet feather appeared. So I just flew behind Udghoshak and landed behind the golden bush when you all were not looking."

"Oh," said Siya.

"And by the way Siya," said Anika, "**What's the secret'** mission completed successfully!" she exclaimed, as the girls did a high five.

Within five minutes, they five were standing at the dark gloomy doorstep of Siya's storeroom (five in the sense- Siya, Abhilash and Anika, who were still too excited to go back to their homes, Udghoshak, who was nudging them to go hurry back to their homes, and Maya, who was still tremendously apologizing for her great mistake and congratulating for their impressive victory against the demon ...*I am deeply ashamed and extremely sorry for my unforgivable lapse of identification...I don't have words to express thou greatness and bravery...I know that the inaccuracy I have shown to thee is highly embarrassing...I have never seen such great warriors like thee in my entire lifetime...*).

"BUH-BYE!" said Udghoshak, pushing Siya, Anika and Abhilash out of the storeroom and pleading Maya to shut up for a second.

The three waved final goodbyes and stepped outside the storeroom.

"How will we lock the door?" asked Siya, looking at the lock which was lying on the floor just the way they had left it, with Siya's hairpin drived into it like a key. "We still don't have the key. Do you know how to lock the key with a hairpin, Anika?"

"We can use magic now," reminded Abhilash. "We have spent a lot of time learning spells," he said,

Siya tried to lock the door using the will of magic, which proved to be quite ineffective on earth, and then tried doing it with the help of her her bluestone, which proved to be just as useful as it had been in Jadooi Jahan. The lock was back on the door, as neatly as it had done yesterday.

"Come to my room," Siya insisted to Anika and Abhilash, as they came back from the gloomy corridors to the brightly lit house. "It's just five thirty now. There's still time for my parents to return."

"Hey! I forgot my diary milk silk there," said Abhilash mournfully, voraciously scrambling in his pockets. Just then, there was a faint familiar groaning sound of engine in Siya's ears.

"What?" asked Anika, as they walked up the stairs to Siya's room. "Why are you looking so alarmed?"

"Hurry!" said Siya in a panickstricken voice. "Dad and Mom are early!"

"What will we do?" asked Anika, frightened, as the engine's croaking neared.

"I wish we could just disappear from here and appear directly in our homes," said Abhilash. "But that was not possible even in Jadooi Jahan!"

"I wish we could become invisible," said Anika.

And don't invite friends. Not when there's no one in the house...And I also don't like it much... Siya could clearly hear her mom's warning.

"Go up to my room!" ordered Siya.

"What?" asked Abhilash unbelievably.

"Just go up!" Siya hissed, and the two sprinted up the curvrd staircase.

Siya heard the car engine stop wailing, and rushed to pen the door. "I heard you coming," she said to her parents with a smile, who were taking out the luggage from the car.

"Oh Siya!" said Mrs. Sharma, bringing a trolley inside the house. "I have been so much worried for you." She abandoned the trolley on the floor and gave a tight hug to Siya. "Did you feel lonely?"

"No," said Siya. "I was fine."

"My brave girl," said Mr. Sharma, landing the other two baggages on the floor, as Siya flung her arms around him and he hugged her back.

"How is Grandma?" she asked.

"Better," replied Mrs. Sharma. "The doctor says that she will be perfectly healthy by tomorrow."

"That's great!" said Siya. "I knew she would be well. Well, I was reading an interesting story," she lied. "So I will be back to my room. I want to know what happens next." Mrs. Sharma gave her a warm smile, as Siya rushed upstairs.

"What will we do now?" asked Anika, as Siya opened the door and closed it abruptly.

"I have thought about that," said Siya.

"What's the plan?" asked Abhilash. Siya pointed at the window. Abhilash peered down through the window, and then stared at Siya as if she had gone mad. "What are you planning? Do you want me to jump from here and go to the hospital with all my bones broken?"

"No," said Siya, as she went to open the window. "You will not jump down. You will walk down," she said, and clutched her bluestone with closed eyes. Just as she did so, stairs appeared at the window, leading to the house's backyard.

"That was clever," said Anika, grinning at Siya. "Come on Abhilash, quick," she insisted as she carefully walked down the stairs, making sure that Mrs. Sharma by no chance was looking at the backyard from any window.

Siya made the stairs disappear as soon as Anika and Abhilash had landed on the ground safely, hoping that her mom come to her room now. She watched from her window as they crept out of the backyard with Anika's cycle throught the backdoor.

Siya thanked her luck that Mrs. Sharma had't happened to know anything that might upset herself. She opened her cupboard and brought out her diary. Then she went to her bed, and began writing-

15ᵗʰ October, 2012

5:45

Dear Diary,

All that which happened between today and yesterday was so exciting, that it's hard to believe. This was the best nightout I have ever had in my whole life ...

...She wrote and wrote and wrote...and went on writing until Mrs. Sharma stalked to her room and switched off the room's light and scolded, "Is this the time you go to sleep? Want to be late for the schoolbus again?"

But Siya's habit of disobedience had never worn off. As soon as Mrs. Sharma had gone out of the room and well out of reach, she tiptoed to the light swotch, switched it on, and started writing again.

And the next day's story was the same as any other day. "Bye mom!" said Siya, and rushed for her school bus. Again she was late today, as usual. Somehow she caught the bus. "Caught it at the last moment," she said panting.

FROM THE AUTHOR'S ⟨

Dear Readers,

First of all, thank you very much for buying this novel and reading it. And secondly, if question be asked about how I came to write this book, then the simple answer is that it's one of my innumerable hobbies to read and write.

I was fourteen when I started writing this novel. And today, at the age of fifteen, I'm glad that my first novel is complete and published. I hope against hope that you found this novel interesting and didn't get bored by it. So ... I think that's all I needed to say. And lastly, thank you again for taking out your precious time to buy my book and go through my story. Because believe it or not, it means a lot to me.

Yours sincerely

Jijnasa Sahani